HORACE
&
BUNWINKLE
THE CASE OF THE RASCALLY RACCOON

Also available by PJ Gardner

Horace & Bunwinkle

PJ GARDNER

HORACE
&
BUNWINKLE
THE CASE OF THE RASCALLY RACCOON

ILLUSTRATIONS BY
DAVID MOTTRAM

BALZER + BRAY
An Imprint of HarperCollins*Publishers*

Balzer + Bray is an imprint of HarperCollins Publishers.

Horace & Bunwinkle: The Case of the Rascally Raccoon
Text copyright © 2021 by PJ Switzer
Illustrations copyright © 2021 by David Mottram

Library of Congress Control Number: 2021937009
ISBN 978-0-06-294657-7

Typography by Laura Mock
21 22 23 24 25   PC/LSCH   10 9 8 7 6 5 4 3 2 1

First Edition

🦴 ♡ 🦴

*To Namina—brilliant critique partner,
fantastic writer, and amazing friend—I'm so
glad we're on this publishing journey together!*

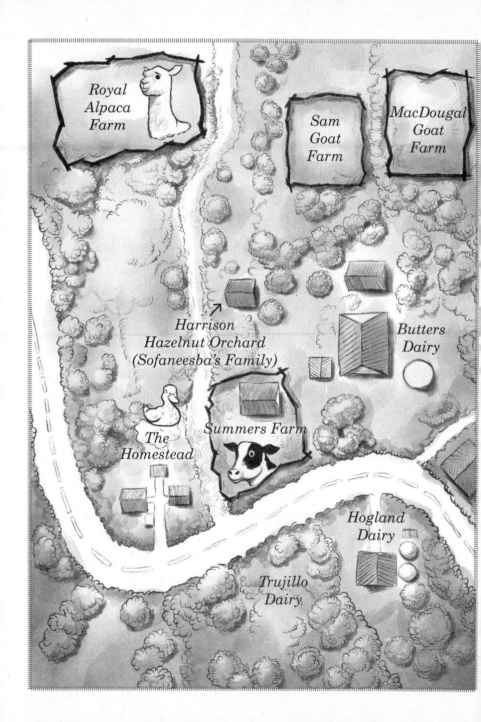

1

Garbage, Garbage Everywhere

Winkie was bored silly. Ellie—that was her human—was busy in her office with something called bills, and Horace—that was her brother—was asleep on the couch next to her.

Horace wasn't her blood brother, on account of him being a dog and her being a pig, but they were still family. The kind of family who loved each other no matter what, even when one of them picked a TV show, then immediately fell asleep and didn't even watch. And then his poor sister had to sit through the boringest show ever, about dogs eating toast.

She looked over at Horace, who was drooling on the couch, and made up her mind. The TV was hers. Winkie slowly put a hoof on the remote. There was no movement from the slobber king beside her. Next she pushed the up arrow. A lady's smiling face appeared on the screen and said, "This lipstick will change your life."

Ugh. No, thanks. Lipstick was the worst. Winkie had worn some not long ago, and it took forever to come off.

Winkie pushed the arrow again and a tall man with a furry scarf appeared.

"Welcome to *Weird and Wonderful.* I'm your host, Sheridan Simper, and this little lady is Jojo." The scarf moved, and a pair of beady eyes stared out of the TV. "Jojo is a lemur, and tonight we're going to explore her homeland, Madagascar."

Ooo, this looked good.

Winkie snuggled down to watch, which was the exact moment Horace started to snore. It was kind of a whistle and kind of a snort and it was kind of driving her crazy. Winkie turned up the TV. Horace got louder. She turned it up again and he got louder again. Finally she put her hoof over Horace's nose-hole to stop the noise.

Yes! Now she could hear the TV.

She pulled her hoof back and got comfortable.

Sheldon handed Jojo an orange. "Lemurs are big fans of fruit. That's because they're herbivores."

Snore.

Agh, seriously?

"They're also highly intelligent. Using tools and doing simple math are no sweat for these primates."

Sno-o-o-o-o-o-ore.

Winkie did the hoof-on-the-nosehole trick again, but as soon as she covered one nosehole, the other one made the noise. It was like she was playing an instrument.

Dang it! Her show would be over before she could turn off Horace's sniffer.

There was only one thing to do—hooves of steel. It was a move she'd borrowed from a character on her favorite TV show, *Andie's Adventures.* Suey was a pig like Winkie, and she solved mysteries with a dog just like Horace. Only Spot didn't snore or talk about New England constantly.

That was where she and Horace had gotten the idea to be pet-tectives. They were good at it too.

Just last week they'd caught a pair of pet thieves who were rounding up animals from the neighborhood. Mostly because of Winkie, but Horace had helped . . . a little. Things had been quiet since then, but she had a feeling that was about to change.

Horace's nose squeaked again.

That was it! Winkie reared up on her hind legs and shouted, "HOOVES OF STEEL!"

Her feet hit Horace on his side.

"You'll never get me to talk, you disgusting fowl you," he grumbled, but his eyes stayed closed.

No way—he was still asleep! And she'd hit him as hard as she could too. Maybe if she did it again, it would work. Winkie got up on her back legs again and . . .

CLANG!

. . . fell right off the couch.

"What the heck?" Winkie squeaked.

Horace just twitched and mumbled in his sleep. "Ducks. Terrible ducks."

How could he sleep through that?

"Hey, something happened in the courtyard."

She nudged him with her snout. "Pet-tectives investigate?"

Horace's noseholes squealed.

"Fine," she said. "I'll go by myself." She clicked her front hooves together. "Pet-*tective*, investigate!"

Winkie didn't understand why Ellie called the space between the house and the barn "the court-yard." That made it sound fancy, but it was really just a gravel driveway. And right now it was a mess.

The trash cans had been knocked over, and the lid to the recycling bin was on the ground next to them. Garbage was everywhere. Empty bottles mixed with used straw from the chicken coop, smeared with Ellie's attempts at cheese making. It was all jumbled together in a big, disgusting wreck.

"Somebody's gonna be in a lot of trouble."

Winkie was almost certain she heard a snort.

"Is someone there?"

Silence.

"Horace?"

She listened extra hard this time. But it was quiet.

Hmm. Maybe she had imagined it.

Then the wind changed direction and an awesome stench filled her snout. There was nothing better than the smell of hot garbage! She grinned. It was Winkie time!

She backed up, then ran, fast as she could, straight into a pile of food scraps. Popcorn, yum!

It was a little soggy, but it still tasted good. Ooo, uncooked pasta—and it was still crunchy! She rooted around and found some grapes and . . . a cloth diaper? Yuck. What was that doing in there?

"You'd better hope Eleanor doesn't catch you

doing that," Horace said in his snootiest voice.

Winkie gasped in surprise, accidentally sucking a grape down her windpipe.

"Agh." She coughed and hacked until her eyes watered. Horace was going to have to do hooves of steel on *her* pretty soon.

Luckily she got the grape out before that happened.

"Good heavens!" Horace patted her on the back. "Are you all right?"

She took a deep breath and nodded, then bent her head to lick up the grape again.

"What are you doing?" he asked suspiciously.

"Getting my food."

Horace kicked it away. "You can't do that. It's covered in drool and dirt."

Winkie chased after the grape. "Tastes good to me."

Horace looked around. "Did you make this mess because you were hungry?"

"I didn't do this."

He hmphed at her.

"No, real—"

"Bunwinkle Irene Higgins! What have you

done?" Ellie's voice came out high-pitched, like a bird's.

Over in the hutch the chicks panicked and screamed, "VULTURE!"

Uh-oh. Winkie was in for it now. Maybe if she looked all sorry and stuff Ellie wouldn't get too mad. Winkie made the saddest face she could and peeked up. But her human wasn't buying it.

"Oh, little pig, I do not have time for any of your antics right now. I've got a job interview at the feed store in fifteen minutes and I can't be late. I *need* this job." Ellie grabbed Winkie and held her at arm's length. "You're going to have to stay in one of the outdoor pens until I get back."

"Aw, not the outdoor pens."

Horace tsked. "Serves you right for knocking over the garbage."

She stuck out her tongue at him. He couldn't see, but it still felt good to do it.

"Hey, Eleanor." An older lady with curly gray hair stood by the gate. "I brought that recipe for ya. Don't know how well it will work with goat cheese, but you're welcome to . . . well, for gosh sakes, would you look at that!"

Horace moved between Ellie and the lady. "Stranger danger!" he barked loudly.

The lady didn't look dangerous to Winkie. She looked like someone's grandma, with big earrings shaped like the letter *B* and a funny T-shirt too. It said ASK ME ABOUT MY KOALIFICATIONS. And the *O*s were koala heads.

"Horace, stop that. This is our friend," Ellie scolded. In a friendlier tone she said, "Sorry, Ms. Butters, I have to take care of something right now."

Okay, that hurt. Winkie was not a something. She was a piglet. And nobody needed to take care of her. They just needed to let *her* take care of the garbage. And by "take care of," she meant eat it.

The butter lady waved her hand. "Stop with that Ms. Butters business. Call me Betty. And let me help. I'll tidy this up while you take care of your animals." She squatted down and started tossing stuff into the trash bin. "Cheese and crackers, your piglet made a heck of a mess."

Winkie turned to glare at the woman . . . and slithered right out of Ellie's hands. She landed, tummy first, on the rocks. For a second she couldn't breathe.

"Oh, little one, I'm so sorry," Ellie bent down and ran a hand over Winkie's head. "Are you okay?"

Horace zoomed to her side. "It's all right. Simply close your eyes and count to ten. It will help you relax."

Count to ten? How was that gonna help her breathe? She needed air, not math.

On top of everything else, Winkie's snout itched like crazy and she couldn't scratch it because she was gonna pass out. She closed her eyes with a whimper.

Out of nowhere a little girl called out, "Pigella Pigerina, are you okay?"

Winkie's eyes snapped open.

Freckles.

Braids.

Overalls.

The Hogland twins!

Winkie's heart started to pound, and she felt dizzy. Suddenly she was caught up in a memory—running in the tall grass behind the barn, small hands gripping her sides, bumping against the ground inside a dark bag. It was like the twins were pignapping her all over again.

"NO!" she squealed. She hopped to her feet and ran before the girls could get her.

"Bunwinkle!" Horace and Ellie called after her.

She would probably get in more trouble now, but it didn't matter. Winkie had to get someplace safe. Someplace she could hide. The barn! There were plenty of places to hide in there.

Fast as a cheetah, Winkie raced inside—and ran snout first into a bale of hay. She fell back on her haunches and blinked her eyes.

Ow, that really hurt. So did her heart. It was beating way too fast.

Something moved beside her, making her squeal again.

"Och, yer doin' it wrong. If ye're goin' to haid-butt somethin', ye've got to do it with the *top* of yer noggin'."

Mal the billy goat stared at her from his pen a few feet away. Winkie shook her head. It was like he wasn't even speaking English.

The sounds of pounding feet and shouting made her scramble up and squirm between a couple bales of hay. Maybe it would be too dark in the barn for them to spot her. Her body shook like Jell-O. She closed her eyes.

"Bunwinkle?" Ellie's voice sounded worried.

"What a cute name for a pig!" Great. The koala lady was there too.

Something tickled Winkie's noseholes. She opened her eyes to see her brother dog's frowning face.

"The twins! Don't let them take me!" Her voice came out high and whiny.

Horace tilted his head, a worried look on his face. "It's all right. No one is going to take you anywhere."

"Pigella, where are you?" one of the girls called out.

Winkie squeaked, "Please, don't let them—"

Mal cut her off with a fierce shout. "Och, ye've come back, ye wee scunners! Ye'll not be taking me again." Then he smashed his head into the gate of his pen.

That's right! The twins *had* petnapped Mal and a bunch of other animals too. But how come he was angry and she was scared?

The twins screamed and jumped back into Betty, who bumped into Ellie, who fell sideways, ramming her shoulder into the shelf next to Smith's stall. Everything—radio, Ellie, and shelf—crashed to the ground.

After that, the barn got really wild. The horses freaked out about their radio, the nanny goats cackled at the chaos, and Winkie shivered like it was January.

What was wrong with her?

An hour later Winkie lay on her piggy bed, snuggled under a blanket, still asking herself the same question. The twins were long gone. They'd hightailed it out of there after Mal had tried to attack. Betty Butters had helped pick up the garbage so

Ellie could get to her interview.

Horace was stretched out next to her, licking his legs. He hadn't said much since everything had happened in the barn, but he would. It was just a matter of time.

"Ah-hem." He cleared his throat.

Winkie tensed up. Here it came—the lecture about misbehaving and keeping a stiff upper lip. Whatever that meant.

Horace turned to look at her. "You appear to be feeling better."

"What?"

"You stopped shaking," he said, "and you're able to focus again."

She turned pink. "Oh yeah. I'm totally focused now. I was out of it earlier 'cause I couldn't breathe."

There was a long pause while Horace stared at her. Time to change the topic.

"Hey," Winkie said, "do you think Ellie is really going to get another job?

He sighed. "She does seem concerned about bills a great deal lately."

It was Winkie's turn to sigh. She'd only asked

the question to distract her brother, but now she was worried.

"And she talks about how much everything costs all the time."

Horace stood tall and said, "Clearly she needs our help." His voice got all snooty, like it always did right before he started talking about New England. "We will find ways to be thrifty and we will be on our best behavior. No more eating food that doesn't belong to us." He gave her a pointed look, then continued. "No more shenanigans. And definitely no more tipping over trash cans."

"I didn't tip anything."

A knock at the door made her jump.

2

A Masked Bandit

Horace's ears perked up at the knock.

Bunwinkle squealed, "They're back!" and buried herself under a pile of blankets.

"Don't worry. No one will get past me!" Horace barked.

There was another knock, and a man's voice called out, "Eleanor, are you there? It's Dean."

Oh, not again. What critical alpaca-related information did Dean need to give Eleanor this time? He had already been to visit four times in the last week. There couldn't possibly be anything left to say about the animals, even for an alpaca rancher like Dean. The man was clearly up to something. As far as Horace was concerned, Dean needed to walk right back through the fields that connected their houses and stay on his own property.

A moment later Dean's face appeared in the window next to the door. He pushed his little round glasses up and scanned the room until he spotted Horace on the leather chair.

"Hey there, little guy, you protecting your home?" He smiled. "So much ferocity in such a small body."

Horace could hear Bunwinkle's muffled laughter behind him.

Dean glanced around some more. "Where's your sister? Is she being a scaredy-cat?"

"Hey!" Bunwinkle squeaked.

Horace would have smiled, but he didn't want the human getting the wrong idea. Instead he barked. Deep, rumbly barks that came out as woofs. The smile fell from Dean's face and he took a step back.

"Calm down, boy. I'm a friend."

A friend? More like a nuisance.

"You're not welcome here!" Horace barked. "Begone with you."

Dean shook his head. "Okay, I'll leave."

Horace stayed at the window, watching as the man walked down the steps and away from the house. Maybe now Dean would take the hint and stay away.

"You can come out. It's safe now," Horace said.

But as he spoke the words, there was a loud

crash from the courtyard. The pile of blankets squeaked and started shaking.

"A trespasser!" Horace stood taller, fierce determination filling his chest. "We must protect the Homestead!"

Another clang drew his attention. The lid to the garbage! Someone was defiling their property. Again. Or maybe that Dean fellow was trying to make trouble.

"Hurry, we have to catch him in the act!"

"Him who?" Bunwinkle asked from under the blankets. "You know what? I don't care. I'm staying here."

"Well, if you don't want to catch the culprit who got you in trouble with Eleanor, that's up to you. But I intend to take this ruffian down and earn a cheese reward."

Horace didn't wait for her to answer. He sprinted for the doggie door, but stopped short of going through it. Only a fool would race into danger without investigating the situation first, and he was no fool. Like Enoch Crosby, New Englander and brave Revolutionary War spy, he would employ stealth and cunning to protect his homeland. Since he was a dog, that meant using his sniffer. He stuck his muzzle through the plastic flaps to smell the air.

Hmm, there was something there—something familiar. But before he could inhale again, Bunwinkle crashed into him from behind. The force pushed him out the doggie door and face-first into a potted plant. The pot rocked back and forth, then settled down. Thank heavens.

"Why did you hit that?" Bunwinkle said in a whisper loud enough for the neighbors to hear. "Now the trespasser knows we're here."

Horace's temper flared. "I hit the pot because of you, you nincompoop." He rubbed his snout. "And if you weren't so loud, we might have snuck up on him."

Bunwinkle huffed. "I didn't—"

He held up his paw to silence her. "We do not have time for a discussion."

The courtyard was silent now, but Horace knew they weren't alone. The scent was stronger out here. The culprit hadn't left.

"We might still be able to catch him," Horace whispered, "but we have to be completely quiet.

And we have to work as a team." He held up a paw. "Pet-tectives investigate!"

Bunwinkle's body began to shake. "I don't know. Maybe this isn't such a good idea. Maybe we should go back in and wait for Ellie."

Horace lowered his paw and stared at her. Even in the dark he could see the fear in her eyes. Something was terribly wrong. It wasn't like her to cower or retreat. She'd been like this all day. Or at least since the incident with the twins earlier.

"If you're scared, you can go back in and wait. I am duty bound as a dog and a New Englander to protect my domain. As General John Stark said, 'Live free or die.'"

Bunwinkle snorted. "Okay, first, I'm not scared. And second, you're just going to check on some trash bandit, not fight the English."

Horace stood up tall. "No matter what I face, I face it with determination."

Her response was another snort.

Ah, that was more like the Bunwinkle he knew.

"Now, let us be stealthy and capture the trespasser."

Slowly they crept forward. Bunwinkle pressed against his side until they reached the trash cans and found them knocked over again.

"I'd better not get blamed for this," she said with a stomp of her hoof.

Suddenly Horace caught a whiff of the familiar smell he'd detected earlier. It emanated from the area right in front of them. They were definitely on the right track.

He put a paw up to his lips. "Shh, we don't want to alert the culprit."

Bunwinkle nodded and put her snout to the ground. "Hmm, smells close." Then, without warning, her head snapped up and she shouted, "We know you're there. Come out with your paws up!"

"What are you doing?" Horace's right eye twitched and he put a paw up to stop it.

"I'm catching the trash bandit. Can't you tell? He's right there."

Horace scanned the contents around the garbage can. The familiar scent was there, but he couldn't see anything out of the ordinary. He turned his attention to the recycling bin next.

Glass bottle, aluminum can, whiskers. Cardboard box.

Wait . . . whiskers?

His eyes flashed back to the spot. Whiskers. And they were attached to a long, thin snout, which was in turn attached to a furry gray face. The face of a raccoon—a rather panicked raccoon, based on the way his beady black eyes darted back and forth between Horace and Bunwinkle.

They stared at each other until Horace cleared his throat and said, "Listen here, rubbish rodent, you need to vacate the premises this instant."

The raccoon squeezed his eyes shut and held his breath.

"What are you doing?" Bunwinkle demanded. "Even if you close your eyes, we can still see you."

The panicky piglet of a few moments earlier had disappeared.

One eye opened, then immediately closed again.

Horace shook his head. This was getting embarrassing. "Sir, please stop playing and remove yourself from our property at once."

There was a great sigh and a clanging of claws

against metal as the creature emerged from between the bins. "This day has been the pits," he said.

He continued talking while he rummaged through the trash.

"First I got chased by animal control. Then someone followed me." He sniffed something he'd found, then tossed it into his mouth. "And now you guys are giving me a hard time."

Good heavens! He was as bad as Bunwinkle.

"What do you think you're doing?" Horace demanded.

"Oh, sorry, it was a squishy grape. Did you want it?"

Horace's spin stiffened. "No," he huffed. "A Boston Terrier does not eat refuse."

"Is that your name? Boston Terrier?" The raccoon wiped his paws on his chest, then curled his right one into a fist and stuck it out. "Name's Shoo."

Bunwinkle covered her snout with both hooves, but Horace could still hear her snickering.

"Boston Terrier isn't a name, it's a breed," he said, ignoring the outstretched paw. "Of course you probably don't know anything about breeds, seeing as you are a mere *Procyon lotor.*"

Shoo lifted his paws in a back-off type of gesture. "Hey now, there's no call for swearing."

"*Procyon lotor* is the Latin name for the common raccoon."

"Cooooollll." The raccoon nodded with a smile. "I dig it. It sounds all mysterious and stuff." Then he winked at them.

Horace's left eye started to twitch now. Why was he always surrounded by weirdos? He closed his eyes and counted to ten. When he opened them again, Bunwinkle was scowling at the raccoon.

"You're the one who made that big mess earlier, aren't you? I got in trouble for that, you know."

"Wasn't me, lil pig. This is all new garbage to me." Shoo winked as he crawled into the garbage can. A moment later a moist paper towel came flying out. It landed on top of Bunwinkle's head.

It was Horace's turn to snicker.

"Stop that!" Bunwinkle shook off the towel and glared at their new friend. "You have to clean this stuff up right now! You can't go around making trouble for other animals."

The raccoon reappeared, a noodle hanging from one ear and a Cheerio stuck to his cheek. He was eating something white and gooey. Horace's stomach turned.

"Do I look like that kind of . . ." He turned to Horace. "What'd you call me earlier, dude? A python locator?"

"It was *Procyon lotor.* And to be perfectly frank, you look exactly like the type of creature to create chaos and walk away."

"I do?" Shoo sounded hurt.

Bunwinkle snorted. "You're standing in our garbage can right now. Of course you're our prime suspect."

Shoo shook his head. "I told you, lil pig, it wasn't me. I spent the day hiding in a tree to keep away from the animal control guy." He took another bite of his gooey treat. "Maybe it was the creeper who was following me."

Bunwinkle rolled her eyes. "Who would follow a raccoon around?"

Horace wasn't sure what to think. Shoo was odd, but he didn't seem like a liar.

"Tell us about the creeper," Horace said.

"You believe him?" Bunwinkle's voice rose in outrage.

"Wore a green jacket, stank like deer wee and cleaning fluid."

"The creeper smelled like deer urine?" Horace asked.

"Totally." Shoo nodded, then his forehead

wrinkled. "Wait . . . no. That was the animal control dude."

Horace sighed loudly.

"And what did the imaginary animal who followed you look like?" Bunwinkle asked, her voice oozing doubt.

"Well, I didn't get a good look at it. I was fighting off some bees. So it was like more of a glimpse. Or, uh, maybe an impression or something."

This creature was ridiculous. Fortunately for them, Horace knew how to handle ridiculous creatures.

"I have an idea," he said. "Close your eyes and relax. We want your mind at ease."

Shoo leaned back on a pile of garbage, and Horace continued. "Take deep cleansing breaths. Let all the tension leave your body."

"Oh, I get it. You want me to tune in to my own inner, cosmic oneness."

Horace rolled his eyes. "Yes, that's exactly what I want. Now empty your thoughts."

"Way ahead of you there, poocherino. My mind is completely blank."

Bunwinkle snorted. "I believe it."

"Yes, good," Horace said, ignoring her comment. "Now think back. Where were you when you caught a glimpse of this other critter?"

"Okay, so it was cool and kind of dark and it smelled like . . . like milk. That's right—there were a bunch of cows around me."

A bunch of cows meant a dairy farm. But there were five of those in the neighborhood. They'd have to narrow it down.

"And what were you doing?" Horace asked.

"Probably digging in garbage and making a mess," Bunwinkle muttered.

Shoo shook his head. "Nah, there's not a lot of trash in a milking shed, and I got an issue with lactose. Besides, I couldn't make a mess, or else they would've found me. I waited there for a while and then, when no one was looking, I hightailed it over to the closest house. That's when I saw the dude. He had a striped tail and dark circles around his eyes."

"A striped tail and dark around the eyes?" Bunwinkle wrinkled her snout. "That's you. You probably caught a glimpse of yourself in a mirror or something."

"Aw, lil pig, that's harsh."

Their conversation was cut off by the sound of Eleanor walking up the road chatting with someone.

"I didn't get the job. And now I have to figure out another way of bringing in more money. I was thinking about using the big field behind the barn for a farmers' market." Eleanor sounded like she was trying to be positive. "My uncle had one years ago, and it was really popular. He rented space to everyone in the neighborhood."

As soon as Shoo heard them, he scrambled out of the garbage and, without another word, scampered across the courtyard. He stopped at the corner of the chicken coop.

For a moment Horace thought he was going to wave or say something, but from the noises Shoo made, it was clear he was being sick.

Then he said, "Gotta lay off the cheese."

His voice hadn't been loud, but it was enough to wake the chicks, who screamed, "Lemur!"

A bright light shone in Horace's face, and Eleanor said, "What do we have here?"

3

Neighbors

Winkie couldn't believe it. Ellie was mad at her again. And all because of that no-good Shoo.

"Again! After everything we went through earlier, you got into the trash *again*?"

"Don't worry about it, El," Dean said, picking up bottles and throwing them in the bin.

"What is he doing here?" Horace grumbled. "I was certain I'd scared him off earlier."

Winkie bumped him with her shoulder. "Maybe he wants to keep Ellie company."

Horace huffed. "He's up to something. Mark my words."

Ellie sighed. "I don't get it. Bunwinkle gets plenty of food. Why does she keep doing this?"

"Don't be too hard on her," Dean said, picking up an empty milk carton and putting it in the bin. "Piglets aren't very mature."

Who was this guy calling immature?

"Still think I'm overreacting?" Horace whispered.

Dean stopped and glanced around. "Besides, I think this is the work of the trash bandit I was telling you about earlier."

"You really think a raccoon did all this?" Ellie asked.

"I do. There's a little guy who's been tearing through the neighborhood for a while. Even got inside my house. It made a mess of my garbage three times before I finally got locks for my bins."

Ellie swung the flashlight back to Winkie and Horace.

"Even if that's true, it doesn't excuse your behavior, missy."

"Oh, they won't do it again." Dean squatted down next them. "They've learned their lesson." He ran a hand down Horace's back. "Haven't you, little fella?"

Horace growled in the back of his throat. Dean

quickly moved his hand over to Winkie's back. "No more pigging out, right, Bunwinkle?"

Then the man had the nerve to bop her on the snout.

Oh, that was it! Winkie looked him in the eyes, then smashed her nose into his.

The next morning Winkie could not get out of bed. It had taken forever to fall asleep. Once she did, she had a bunch of nightmares in a row, including one really bad one where she was trapped in a garbage can and couldn't get out. She called for Horace and Ellie, but no one could hear her. Then a pair of hands grabbed her and stuffed her into a reusable grocery store bag.

She yawned and stretched halfheartedly.

"What an awful night," she mumbled to herself.

"Oh, did you have a bad night?" Horace's voice sounded concerned, but when Winkie rolled over, his expression was all frowny and grumpy.

"I couldn't tell, what with a pair of hooves kicking me in the back every fifteen minutes. I'll probably be bruised for weeks." Horace rubbed a spot near his tail and glared at her.

Winkie glared right back. "That's big talk from a guy who smacks me in the face when he chases dream ducks!"

Horace sat up tall. "I have no idea what you're talking about. However, if I did have such dreams, I'm sure it would simply be my mind attempting to stay alert."

Ooo, that was just like him.

"That's it." Winkie stood up. "I'm moving my bed."

She climbed off her piggy pillow, then grabbed hold of a corner with her teeth and pulled with all her might. It didn't move. Not even an inch. Horace cleared his throat, like he wanted her to look at him, but she refused to turn her head.

This pillow was gonna move if it took all day.

"Breakfast!" Ellie called from the kitchen.

Or not. Winkie instantly let go and headed for her food bowl.

Horace trotted up beside her. "Make sure you eat your own food. Remember, no more waste!"

And he called *her* obnoxious. She turned up her snout and ignored him.

Breakfast was always a bowl of piggy kibble, which was way better than dog kibble. Winkie had tried some of Horace's food when she first came to the Homestead. It wasn't anything special. She'd eaten all of it just to be sure, though.

Ellie sat at the kitchen table making phone calls about her farmers' market idea.

A hard knock on the screen door made Winkie jump. Horace's head shot up from his bowl, a frown on his face. About a second later Winkie got a snout full of the stankiest stink that ever stunk. Her eyes immediately started watering.

"What is that?" She gagged.

Horace winced and put a paw over his nose. "Something dead. No living creature could produce a smell so . . . so . . ." He trailed off.

She totally understood why. Winkie loved a good stench. She liked figuring out what created each part of it. That was why garbage was great. There were all these different bits. But this wasn't a normal smell. The stink that was attacking them now was like a bunch of chemicals got in a fight and decided to make everyone suffer.

Winkie scooted toward the door. She didn't want to get closer to the stench, but she had to know what was making it. Horace scooted with her.

Ellie walked to the screen door, the top of her shirt pulled up to cover her mouth and nose.

"Can I help you?"

The guy on the other side of the screen was dressed in tan pants and a dark green jacket. He nodded at Ellie.

"Good morning, ma'am. My name is Clark Samson, and I work for animal control."

This must be the guy Shoo was talking about.

"I'm going door-to-door in your neighborhood regarding a . . ." He glanced around, then leaned in closer. ". . . certain masked bandit. If you know what I mean."

Ellie sneezed twice and took a step back.

"Sorry about the smell, ma'am, that's my home-made all purpose animal musk. Absolutely vital for my job."

Horace rubbed his sniffer. "Good heavens, I think the stench is actually getting stronger."

"Yeah, that eau de raccoon is burning the hair out of my noseholes," Winkie said.

Samson's eyes got big when he noticed her.

"Oh, ma'am, forgive me for saying this, but it is extremely dangerous to have a pig in the house." He shook his head. "Pigs have been known to suffocate humans in their sleep. It's true. See, they're roamers. They like to move around under the cover of darkness looking for a source of warmth. They find a vulnerable human and lie across the neck."

Horace snorted, then immediately started wheezing.

Winkie's mouth fell open. Big mistake. Now she could *taste* the smell.

"Yes . . . well." Ellie seemed stumped for words.

"It's a fact. Look it up. But that's not why I'm here." The guy pulled a piece a paper of out of his pocket. "I'm pursuing this varmint."

He held it up to the screen so Ellie could see. Winkie's eyesight wasn't the best, but she was pretty sure the photo was just one big blur.

Ellie looked at the photo, then at the guy holding it before she answered. "I haven't seen anything that looks like that."

Samson put the photo back in his pocket and pulled out a notebook. "No sightings," he said as he wrote. "If you see him, please give me a call at . . . you should write this down."

"I don't have a pen handy," Ellie said. "Do you have a business card?"

"Unfortunately, business cards are only given to level-two agents, and I am currently a level three." His face turned red like he was embarrassed. "Therefore, I will write it down for you."

Suddenly he stopped and sniffed the air. "He's near. I can sense it." He sniffed again. "Watching.

Waiting." He turned. "In the field behind that barn. That's where I will face the beast."

With that, he unzipped his jacket and pulled out something that looked like a mini crossbow. "I have to go," he said, then raced down the front stairs.

"What do you think he's going to do with that?" Winkie whispered.

Horace's only answer was another sneeze. It wasn't just any sneeze either. It was the biggest, wettest sneeze ever. And it hit Winkie right in the face.

"Aw, gross, my mouth was open."

"Zo zorry," Horace mumbled.

They were all still standing at the door when Ellie's phone buzzed.

"Hello."

Horace started making a horrible noise that sounded like he was either going to shoot snot out his nose or barf.

Ellie knelt down and patted him hard on the back. "You'll be okay, baby boy, you just need to get that out." Into the phone she said, "Ms. Jamison, I'm so glad you called." She patted Horace's back again. "I was trying to find out the status of my loan. . . . Oh. I was turned down."

Loan? Winkie looked at Horace, but he wasn't paying attention. His *hurk-hurk* noises were getting louder.

"I'm sorry. I'll have to call you back. My dog is having some health issues right now."

Horace didn't barf, but he didn't get better either. Ellie finally had to give him a special medicine for allergies, which made him super tired. He slept the rest of the day. Winkie thought about going outside to look for another mystery to solve or something, but her body started to shake every time, so she settled for watching an *Andie's Adventures* marathon.

They were both a little groggy when they woke up the next morning, so they walked around the Homestead for a while.

As they passed the garage, Horace stumbled over some rotted wood that had fallen off the building.

"Eleanor really needs to fix that," he said with a frown. "It's dangerous."

"I don't think she can," Winkie said. "She didn't get that job, remember. So she probably doesn't have enough money to fix it."

"And, based on the phone call from the bank earlier, she didn't get a loan either." Horace gave a big sigh. "We've got to help Eleanor somehow."

"We need to make money." Winkie said. "I've got it! I'll get a job driving trains. I watched a show about it and it's super easy." She tapped her hooves. "And you can go on a game show. You're a know-it-all, so you'll do great."

"Or we could do patrol duty to keep the field safe so she can have the farmers' market there."

Winkie wrinkled her snout. "My idea was better."

"Now let's go inspect the field and make a plan to protect it." Horace marched off, head up, as if he'd done something amazing.

She tried to follow him, but her feet wouldn't move.

After a few steps Horace turned back to look at her. "Are you coming?"

She nodded, but her body still wouldn't do what her brain was telling it to do. Instead of walking, it started shaking. No! She had been fine a minute ago. What had happened? They were just going to a field. She'd been there loads of times before, and nothing bad had ever happened to her. Except that time she got pignapped.

Don't think about that, Winkie. Think about something happy.

"Why don't you patrol the front of the house?" Horace offered. He said it like it was no big deal, but it was obvious he could tell she was having problems. "I'll inspect the field myself."

"You mean we're going to split up?" She hated that her voice shook, but she couldn't control it.

Horace didn't say anything right away, which just made Winkie more embarrassed. "That's okay. I'm good," she mumbled, forcing her feet to move.

She had gotten halfway across the courtyard when Horace joined her. "Actually, I think two sniffers would be better for this job."

They couldn't detect much in the front of the house because the air was rank with skunk stink. It was almost as bad as that Samson guy's cologne.

"Blast," Horace huffed. "It will take at least an

hour to clear that smell from our sniffers. I suppose we'll simply have to watch the road while we wait."

He was being nice to Winkie again. It bugged her a lot. She wasn't a baby. And she wasn't scared. Not really. She was just . . . off. It was probably the bad dreams from last night making her feel weird.

Right now she was gonna chew on this piece of wood sticking up from the porch and relax. Chewing was what Winkie did when she got nervous. Or excited. Or confused.

She chewed on things a lot.

She had just gotten into the crunch zone when she heard something rustling under the porch.

"Horace . . . I think something's under the—"

He leaned close to her ear and whispered, "Don't say anything else. If it's the skunk, we don't want to startle him."

"Let's get Ellie," she whispered back. "I don't want to get sprayed again."

Horace nodded. "Excellent plan. You leave first and I'll follow."

Winkie made a big deal of yawning and stretching. And then, real loud, she said, "I can't get comfortable out here. I'm going inside."

She winked at Horace, but he didn't wink back. He mouthed the word "Go."

Winkie didn't mean to look, honestly she didn't, but her eyes got curious. They really wanted to know what was under there. She peeked down and found a pair of eyes staring back at her through a hole in the porch.

"Don't make a sound," a voice ordered from below.

4

A Wounded Weirdo

Horace was too startled to do anything more than blink. Bunwinkle, on the other hand, jumped three feet in the air and landed on Horace's back. He collapsed on the porch with a loud thump.

"Will you get off me?" he gasped, once he could breathe again.

She crawled down but stuck close to his side.

"Aw, sorry about that, lil pig. I didn't mean to scare you."

"Shoo?" Horace peered down at the creature staring at them from under the porch. "What are you doing under there?"

"Scaring me to pieces," Bunwinkle grumbled, her face turning pink.

"Yeah." There was a long pause. "Wait, no. Not on purpose anyway. See, I'm in a bit of trouble."

Horace's heart sank. Why was it always trouble? Why didn't anyone ever come to them with cheese and an amusing story?

Bunwinkle narrowed her eyes in suspicion. "What did you do?"

Shoo's face disappeared from sight, and there was a soft thud. "Oof."

That didn't sound good. Horace leaned down and peered through the knothole "Shoo, are you, by any chance, injured?"

"Dude, are you, like, seismic?" Shoo asked in an awed voice.

"You mean psychedelic," Bunwinkle corrected.

The raccoon's eyes got wide. "Whoa, you too, lil pig? You read minds?"

Winkie turned her head away and giggled. "Dang it! I don't want to like him. He got me in trouble with Ellie."

Horace pressed his lips together. There really were no normal animals in this area.

"The word you are both searching for is 'psychic.'" Horace sighed. Then he leaned over and said, "Wait there. We'll be there in a minute."

"We're going under the porch?" Bunwinkle's giggles disappeared.

Horace nodded as he walked down the steps. He didn't trust his voice.

"But you said it was dangerous under there!" Bunwinkle chased after him. "You said it was full of spiders and snakes that could eat us in one bite."

"I'm sure . . . ," he croaked. He cleared his throat. "Ah-hem, I'm sure it's not that bad."

Bunwinkle ran in front of him and blocked his way. "You said that if we went under there, we'd wind up getting shots again. Shots!"

A shudder passed through Horace's body. He detested shots. And how was it that she recalled all his warnings about the porch but couldn't remember which food bowl was hers?

"We have no choice but to risk it."

She stopped him again when they reached the gap in the latticework that served as the entrance. "But you'll get all dirty. You hate getting dirty, Horace."

He had a sudden urge to lick his legs. But if he

stopped now, he might lose his courage.

"That's true." He stood tall and tilted up his muzzle. "But Shoo is hurt, and at the moment we're the only ones who can help him. We simply can't walk away. It's like President John F. Kennedy said, 'Courage—not complacency—is our need today.'"

"Is everybody from New England brave?"

"Yes," Horace answered without hesitation.

Bunwinkle took a deep breath. "Fine. Let's go rescue that silly raccoon."

The underside of the porch was not as bad as he'd feared. There were an uncomfortable number of cobwebs and it was very dirty, but there didn't appear to be anything dangerous like rusty nails or mud. They found Shoo near the front stairs. He was sprawled facedown on his stomach.

"Oh no, he's dead!" Bunwinkle ran to the body.

Shoo's head popped up. "Someone died? Dude, that's so sad. Did I know 'em?"

Bunwinkle bumped him with her snout. "We're talking about *you*."

"I'm dead?" Tears came to the raccoon's eyes.

"But there was so much I wanted to do. So much garbage I wanted to eat."

Horace's right eye started twitching. He took a deep breath to calm himself. Then another one. He really needed to lick his legs, but there wasn't time.

"You're not dead." He was pleased that his voice came out sounding calm and reasonable.

"Oh, thank goodness. My mom would've killed me if I died."

Deep breath, Horace. Take a deep breath and count to ten. You came down here to help this unfortunate creature. Remember that.

Apparently Bunwinkle was struggling to keep

her temper as well. She bopped Shoo on the back with her hoof. "Are you even hurt? We came down here into the creepiest place on the planet to help you, but if you're okay, we're leaving."

Shoo winced. "Careful, lil pig, I scraped my back getting down here."

"Is that all?" Bunwinkle snorted.

"Yeah." Shoo thought about it, then added, "That and my ear. It got bent when I landed on my head."

Horace stepped closer. "You landed on your head?"

"'Cause my tail broke."

Bunwinkle shook her head. "How did your tail break?"

"The dude wouldn't let go of it," Shoo said, as though it should have been obvious.

"What dude?" Bunwinkle sounded as confused as Horace.

"You know, the one who's been chasing me. The one in the green jacket. Smells like a dead carcass. He caught me when I met my evil twin."

Horace was going to regret asking, but he had to know. "Evil twin?"

Shoo's expression turned serious. "Okay, have you ever heard the theory that everyone has a twin out in the world? Someone who looks exactly like you? Well, I saw mine. Actually, it was the second time I saw 'im. Only this time I got a good look. Black circles around the eyes, a striped tail. Real aggro too."

"What does that even mean?" Bunwinkle grumbled.

"He was aggressive. Came at me when I caught him inside this human dude's house."

It was Horace's turn to ask a question. "He was inside someone's house?"

Shoo nodded. "Totally. See, I was sitting in the garbage, which was right next to the house. I was eating some stellar yogurt when I heard something inside. I ducked down in case it was a human, but it was him. He messed around with the dude's computer. I thought maybe he was there to look at videos of rampaging raccoons. There's a funny one where this lil guy gets stuck in a fence and winds up playing ball with a dog. It's a classic."

"Focus," Horace said through gritted teeth.

"Right. But it was weird—he didn't do anything with the computer. Just turned it on and put this black whatchamacallit in the side, then a minute later took it out again. I couldn't see what it was, so I leaned closer to the window, but the trash can rattled and he spotted me. He charged the window—I thought he was going to come through it. Scared me so bad I jerked back. That's when the animal control dude grabbed hold of my tail. I bit the dude's hand without thinking. He screamed and dropped me. I thought I'd be safe in the field across the way, but I ran into a skunk. He chased me over here, trying to spray me. He got your front steps instead. Sorry about that."

Bunwinkle nodded. She'd had a run-in with that particular skunk not long ago as well.

Shoo shook his head sadly. "That guy's got some serious anger issues. And he's way too territorial. I think meditation would help him."

"Psst. Psst."

Horace glanced at the source of the noise—Bunwinkle. She jerked her head toward the entrance, then walked away

"Will you excuse us, Shoo? My partner and I

need to confer for a minute," Horace said.

"Cool, dude. I'm just gonna lie here and center my inner harmonies."

Shoo dropped his head to the ground again and went still. If Horace didn't know better, he would have sworn the raccoon was dead.

"Psst!" Bunwinkle practically shouted.

Horace turned around and followed the sound to the far side of the house.

She leaned close and whispered, "I think there's something wrong with that raccoon."

"Most definitely," he agreed.

"Right? That story sounded like something Jones the horse would come up with. A raccoon playing games on a computer?" Bunwinkle snorted. "Shoo probably ate something funky, saw himself in a mirror, and freaked out."

Horace's eye began to twitch again. "That's not what he said. He told us the raccoon turned on the computer and put something in the side."

"I don't buy it. Why would an animal break into a house and get on the computer? It doesn't make sense."

It *didn't* make sense, and yet Horace didn't

think Shoo had made it up either. He had no reason to.

"Let's speak with him again," Horace said.

"Hmph" was her response.

Despite her doubts, Horace noted that she followed him back to the front of the house. Shoo had
rolled onto his side and was picking his nose and
humming "I'm a Little Teapot."

"I told you something was wrong with him,"
Bunwinkle whispered.

"All this proves is that he's disgusting, and we
already knew that."

Shoo spotted them and waved. "Hey, I know
you guys. What are you doing here?"

Bunwinkle shook her head and muttered the
word "weirdo" under her breath. Aloud she said,
"We're here to help you."

The raccoon smiled at them. "That's awesome.
You dudes are the best friends a guy could have."

"Yes . . . well . . . yes." Horace didn't quite know
how to respond to that statement. "I think we
should get you medical treatment for your injuries. Can you walk?"

"Oh yeah." Shoo stood up and immediately

collapsed again. "Guess not."

"I suppose we'll have to get Eleanor to come to you. I'm not certain she'll fit, though. What do you think, Bunwinkle?"

She gasped, and he turned to look at her. Bunwinkle's eyes had grown round, and even from a distance he could see her shake.

"They trapped us," she whispered.

"No one did any . . ." He trailed off. The spot where they had come in was now blocked by a piece of lattice that had been propped against the stairs when they entered.

Bunwinkle backed away, whispering, "Trapped." She only stopped when her back leg collided with Shoo's head.

"Aw, lil pig, are you coming to give me a hug?" The raccoon opened his arms wide.

A look of confusion passed over her face.

"It's okay," Horace said calmly. "We'll find another way out."

Her eyes darted around wildly. "There isn't another way out. There was just that one spot and now it's . . . it's . . ."

The end of the sentence was cut off by a heavy set of footsteps going up the stairs. A moment later, there was a knock at the back door and Dean's voice called out, "Hey, El, you ready to shear those alpacas?"

"What is Dean doing here *again*?" Horace asked with a frown.

"Who cares?" Bunwinkle snapped. "We're stuck down here!"

Horace held up a paw to quiet her down. "Now, now, would—"

"No." She knocked his paw away. "Don't tell me about some stupid human who was brave or smart or whatever on account of being from New York."

"New England," he corrected automatically.

"WHO CARES?" she screamed, and ran past him.

"Poor lil pig." Shoo hadn't turned his head, so his words came out muffled. "The freak-outs are no fun."

For once Horace had to agree with the odd creature.

5

Hippos or Limes or Rabies, Oh My

Winkie ran around looking for another way out. There had to be a place she could squeeze through, right? She was small—she didn't need much space. But no matter how hard she looked, she couldn't find one. They really were trapped.

"Calm down. It's okay," Horace said. "Ellie's home. All we have to do is make some noise and she'll find us."

That's right. They were home. Ellie would save them.

"Help!" he called, and Winkie joined in.

A few minutes later they heard footsteps approach, but it wasn't Ellie. It was that Butters lady.

"Betty?" That was Ellie's voice. "What are you doing here?"

The lady stood up, and Winkie got a good look at what she was wearing. It was another animal T-shirt. This one had a drawing of a monkey in a paper coffee cup, and on the cup it said I'LL HAVE A CAPUCHIN-O. Winkie would have giggled if she weren't so upset.

"I think your pets are trapped under your house." Betty pointed at them.

They heard scrambling, and then their human was staring at them through the lattice. "How did you get down there?" She tugged on the wood, but it didn't budge.

Dean suddenly appeared next to her. "That's my fault. I moved this piece of lattice so that skunk wouldn't get under there. I'm sorry." He shifted something on one end, and the lattice came right off.

Winkie ran straight into Ellie's arms. The shaking came back worse than before, which didn't make any sense. She was safe now.

"Thank goodness you found them," Ellie said, hugging Winkie tight.

Betty waved her hand. "Gosh sakes, it was nothing. I just followed the ruckus, and there they were."

Ellie shifted as though she was going to set Winkie down, but Winkie wasn't ready. She squealed and scrambled closer.

Dean knelt down beside them. "El, I think something is wrong with her. She's acting strange."

Winkie glared up at him.

"She's up-to-date on her rabies shot, right?" Betty asked, pulling her hand back from Winkie's head.

What? She didn't have rabies. She was just a little freaked out.

"I think so," Ellie said. "But it doesn't look like rabies to me. She's not drooling or making weird noises."

Betty cleared her throat. "You know, when I worked at the county zoo we had a saying. 'Ya can't tell a hippo is pregnant just by looking at her.'"

Wait, was this lady calling Winkie a hippo?

Dean said what everyone was thinking. "I don't get it."

"It means there's a lot you can't see until you have the vet check them out," Betty clarified.

Ellie frowned. "Them?"

"If she does have rabies, there's a good chance the dog would too, since they've been together."

Dean sighed. "I don't think it's rabies, but it could be blastomycosis or Lyme disease. It's better to be safe."

So now Winkie was going to turn into a lime? What was going on?

Ellie didn't waste any time after that. She had her phone out and was talking to the vet in less than a minute.

"Okay, right. Seven a.m. tomorrow." She hung up the phone and squeezed Winkie close to her.

"Maybe you should cancel the farmers' market meeting tonight," Dean said, putting his hand on Ellie's shoulder. "It might not be a good idea to have a bunch of people over to your house right now."

Horace glared at him and gave a low, rumbly growl.

"Oh, don't do that," Betty said. "Let me help. That's why I came over in the first place—to volunteer. We can work on a proposal together and I'll host the meeting."

"Are you sure? I don't want to take up your time." Ellie sounded hopeful.

"Honey, since I retired from the zoo, all I've got is time."

"What about the dairy?" Dean asked. "Doesn't Bertie need you to help her?"

Betty shook her head. "Mom's got it all under control. Besides, she's not interested in any of my silly little ideas."

"Well, I'd be grateful for the help," Ellie said. "I can barely keep up with the Homestead as it is."

Without warning, Betty scooped Horace off the ground. "Let's get these two to a safe place, and then we can talk about the meeting."

Ellie struggled to stand, and the next thing Winkie knew, she was in Dean's arms. "I've got her, El."

Horace woofed loudly as Betty walked to the outdoor animal pens. Where was she going? Didn't she realize they were *pets*?

"Oh no, they don't stay out here," Ellie said.

Betty nodded but still set Horace down in the

gated area. "I hate to say this, but it's safer for you if they're out here, at least until you know for sure they don't have rabies."

"I'm sure it's nothing serious, El. These two act weird all the time, right?" Dean patted Ellie on the shoulder.

How did he do it? How did he always manage to say the exact wrong thing?

Winkie hoped Ellie would save them and say they could go watch TV on the couch. But she didn't. She just gave them a sad look and said, "This is for the best, little ones."

"Ridiculous!" Horace looked mad enough to spit nails. "We don't have rabies. I'm merely dirty from being under the house, and you are . . . uh . . . a bit . . . discombobulated."

"Yeah." Winkie stomped her hoof. "Is debobcatted when you shake a lot and small spaces make you freak out?"

Horace opened his mouth, paused as if he was thinking about something, and then said, "Exactly. And now poor Eleanor will have to pay another vet bill. This is the exact opposite of what we were trying to do."

This was all Shoo's fault.

"Now, Dean, you head on home while Eleanor and I make our plans."

As soon as the humans left, Winkie's nose started itching. Ah, not again.

Once they were gone, Horace turned to Winkie with a frown. "Are you feeling better now?"

Winkie's face got hot. She'd acted like a big baby when they were trapped, and she'd said mean things to her brother. "Sorry for what I said. I didn't mean it." Hopefully he'd drop the subject now.

He didn't drop it.

"I understand. You were scared and—"

"I'm fine. Really." Which was true, now that she was out from under the house.

Winkie had never been so glad to see the Schott, Schwink, & Schwank mobile veterinary van in her life. The outdoor pens were the boringest place in the world, and they'd been stuck there for a whole afternoon and night. Plus, Ellie had kind of freaked Winkie out. She'd checked on them every half hour and then, after all that talk with Betty Butters, she wound up rescheduling the farmers' market meeting so she could be home with them. Winkie couldn't wait to see Dr. Schwank, prove she didn't have rabies, and go back to her spot on the couch.

But Dr. Schwank didn't get out of the van. It was a red-haired man who opened the door—Dr. Shot.

Winkie sighed. "I guess we're getting shots."

"Curse whoever brought up rabies," Horace said.

The vet's examination was quick. Mostly it involved squishing Winkie's body, checking her mouth, and making her walk around. No big deal. Until the end, when the red-haired jerk caught her up close to his body and said, in the high-pitched little-girl voice that he used with animals, "This won't hurt a bit."

Well, it definitely didn't hurt *him*.

He put Horace through the same thing. When he was finished, Dr. Shot grinned his super-big grin. "I don't think they have rabies, but I gave them another vaccine, just in case. There haven't been any cases reported in the area that I know of. Although animal control did stop by to tell us they were looking for a suspicious raccoon."

Shoo had rabies! Winkie knew it. Well, she hadn't exactly known it was rabies, but she'd known something was wrong with him.

Dr. Shot packed up his medical bag. "I hope it's not true. It's such a sad end to those poor critters."

What did he mean by "sad end"? An image of the little crossbow that the animal control guy had popped into her mind.

"Now, about the bill," the vet said.

Ellie sighed. "Can I do a payment plan? I'm afraid I can't pay the whole bill right now."

Winkie stopped listening. She felt like the air had been knocked out of her. But what if Shoo didn't have it? They wouldn't hurt him then, right?

"This is a catastrophe," Horace whispered to her. "We've got to do something."

"Yeah, we gotta get him somewhere safe."

Unfortunately, Ellie herded them into the house and closed the pet door so they could only go outside when she was there to watch over them. They waited all day for a chance to move Shoo, but it never came. Ellie locked them in the house while she worked around the Homestead in the morning, then sat with them in the living room, chatting on the phone with Ms. Butters and Clary Hogland until she took off for her meeting around 8:30 p.m.

After she left, they counted to one hundred before they set their plan in motion.

"Before we start, we have to do the thing," Horace said.

"What thing?"

He held up his paw. "You know. Pet-tectives investigate."

Winkie tilted her head in confusion. "But we're not investigating anything."

"I've been thinking about that. I believe there's more to this business with Shoo than meets the eye. There are a number of questions that need to be answered. For instance, who was that other critter that charged at Shoo? Why was it in someone's house? And what was it doing on the computer?"

"You actually believe Shoo about all that?"

Horace got that "New Englanders are the best" look on his face and nodded. "I do."

"Fine." Winkie sighed. "We'll investigate." She rolled her eyes but held out her hoof for Horace to bump.

"Pet-tectives investigate!" they said in unison.

"Now can we get out of the house?"

The first step was to lift the plastic panel on the pet door. Winkie would press the button on the side while Horace pushed the door up with a tool of some kind.

"What can we use?" Horace asked. "It has to be sturdy but thin."

Winkie glanced around and noticed an old pitcher full of wooden spoons on the kitchen table. "Hey, what about one of those?"

Horace shook his head. "Absolutely not. It would require one of us to get on the table, and that is against the rules. Besides, Eleanor worked very hard on that centerpiece. She'd definitely notice if one of the spoons went missing."

"No, she wouldn't. And besides, Shoo's life is at stake. We don't have a choice."

A pained look crossed his face. "Fine, but I'll be the one to do it. Who knows what sort of mess you'd make?"

She'd actually been feeling sorry for him until that last bit.

Horace hopped up on a chair and put his paws on top of the table. He stayed like that for a minute. Then more minutes. Winkie waited patiently. And then not so patiently.

"Horace! We don't have time for this. Ellie will only be gone for an hour."

"I . . . I can't do it." He took his paws off the table and sat down on the chair. "I'm a good boy. I follow the motto of President John Adams. 'To be good, and to do good, is all we have to do.'"

If this kept up, they'd never make it out of the house.

"Yes, but think about it. You're doing a small bad thing in order to do a super-big good thing."

Horace nodded. "I suppose that is true. And it's not like I enjoy breaking the rules. I'm merely doing so in aid of a fellow creature."

"Exactly," Winkie agreed with him. Although at this point she'd have agreed with anything he said as long as it got him moving.

"Yes, this is the right thing to do," he said as he continued to sit on his butt.

"Please, Horace, just do it."

He took a deep breath, closed his eyes, and gingerly stepped onto the table. "I don't feel right about this. I should get down."

"GET THE SPOON!"

It took six bajillion years, but Horace finally did it. And then they were at the pet door.

"Remember, you have to push the button all the way in or the door won't move," Horace told her for the third time.

"Got it. Now let's do this."

"Un, tuh, fwee." Horace counted down for them, spoon in his mouth.

Miracle of miracles, it worked—the door slid up.

Winkie smiled. "Easy peasy, snacks and cheesy."

They crept out with their sniffers on high alert—it would ruin everything if they got caught before they could get Shoo. Winkie couldn't force herself to go under the porch again, and Horace didn't make her. She kept a lookout while he went in. But Shoo wasn't there.

"Where do you think he went?" Winkie asked Horace after he crawled out from under the house.

Horace sniffed the air. "I think he's in the trash again."

"He'd better not be making another mess." She stomped her hoof.

They found Shoo wedged between the garbage and recycling cans, drinking water out of a plastic bottle and making weird noises. Horace walked toward him, but Winkie got in the way.

"Wait a second. Before we go over there, should we maybe put on some kind of protective gear in case he does have rabies?"

Horace paused, frowning. "But he didn't have any signs."

He started walking again, and Winkie got in the way again.

"There were lots of signs. Dr. Shot checked to see if I could walk normal, if I was confused, and if I made odd noises. When Shoo tried to walk, he fell over. He keeps using weird words like 'aggro,' and he's making odd noises right now." Winkie jerked her head toward Shoo, who was honking and snorting.

"I have an idea." Horace went back under the house and came out with the wooden spoon.

Together they walked over to the trash bins. Shoo's head drooped to one side and his tongue stuck out of his mouth. When they were close enough, Horace poked Shoo in the belly with the end of the spoon.

The raccoon's head snapped up. "Hey!"

Winkie squealed, and Horace dropped the spoon with a yelp.

"Oh, wow, I must have fallen asleep."

She took a deep breath through her noseholes. This critter was too much.

Shoo waved. "Seriously, dude, it is so good to see you and lil pig. I was sure I'd be stuck here forever. I mean, it's not a bad place to be stuck, but my back is killing me. And I'm gonna need to find a private spot where I can give back to nature, if you know what I mean."

Winkie shook her head in disgust. Too much information.

Horace stopped a few feet away from the garbage bins. "Yes, I know what you mean. But before we address that issue, Bunwinkle and I need to be sure you're all right."

"Yeah, we gotta check you for rabies."

"Oh, I don't have any babies," Shoo said, his face totally serious. "I'm not ready to settle down yet."

"Rabies!" Winkie shouted at him. She turned to Horace and said, "I'd call that confusion."

"Yes, but it might have something to do with

that." Horace pointed at Shoo's ear. Something was sticking out of it.

"So he's got hairy ears."

Horace snorted. "That's not hair. I believe it's some sort of vegetable. Shoo, is there something stuck in your ear? Shoo?"

"Huh?"

Winkie glared at the varmint. How could anybody be this clueless?

"Your ear! There's something in it!" Horace shouted.

This was almost as bad as talking to Smith, the old horse who pretended to be deaf.

"Your ear!" Winkie shouted with Horace.

Shoo's face scrunched up in confusion. He scratched his head like he was trying to figure out what they were saying. His paw must have touched the greens, because his expression went from confused to excited.

"Whoa, dude," he said, removing the stuff. "Check it out—I had a radish in my ear." He held it up for them to see. "No wonder I couldn't hear you."

"Still think he's not confused?" Winkie

whispered loudly.

Horace pressed his lips together as they watched the raccoon sniff his ear radish, then take a bite of it. "I'm fairly certain that's his natural state."

She watched as Shoo took another bite of ear radish, then started singing.

"You may be right. But he was walking funny."

"Because he had a head injury," Horace said, "and a broken tail."

That's right, Shoo had said that. "Well, what about that chicka, chicka, chick noise he was making?"

Shoo perked up. "That's a great song, isn't it? Nobody sings harmony like Guys 'R' Great."

Guys 'R' Great? What was that?

"Actually, I prefer the group Five 4 One,"

Horace said, totally avoiding Winkie's eyes.

What was he even talking about? She stared at him until he cleared his throat and said, "They're boy bands. 'Chicka, Chicka' is a lesser-known song by Guys 'R' Great. I thought I recognized it, but I wasn't certain until he said something."

"I was in a video with the Guys when I was a kit," Shoo said. "You know the one where they all dressed like farm critters? They filmed it just up the road."

For the first time in probably her whole life, Winkie couldn't think of anything to say. Horace liked boy bands, and the raccoon was a video star. She sat back on her haunches and closed her eyes. Nothing made sense anymore.

"Does this mean Shoo really saw some critter breaking into houses?" she asked, not expecting an answer.

Shoo nodded. "Sure does, and he's over there looking in your window right now."

6

Home Invasion

Horace's mouth fell open. He hadn't truly believed the story about another raccoon bandit. But he couldn't deny it when he saw a ringed tail—barely visible in the fading light—disappearing around the side of the house.

"No way!" Bunwinkle gasped. She opened her mouth to say more, but Horace put his paw over it.

"Shh, we want to sneak up on him, and we can't do that if you give away our position."

She rolled her eyes.

"If I remove my paw, you can't be loud."

Her answer was to lick his paw. He pulled it back and wiped it on the ground. "How immature."

Bunwinkle tapped her feet in panic. "He's gonna get away."

He stood tall. "Not if I have anything to say about it."

"Right!" Her eyes grew round. "I've got your back, brother."

Horace stared at her, careful to keep the concern he was feeling hidden.

They scurried up the stairs quickly and quietly, then edged along the side of the house until they reached the corner. Horace peeked around the corner. The sun had set, making it harder to see, but he was certain the critter was still close by—a peculiar scent lingered.

"It's weird. He doesn't smell like Shoo," Bunwinkle whispered.

He nodded. "I don't understand it either, but that distinctive smell works to our advantage. He'll be easier to track."

They followed the scent along the edge of the house, then around front, then back down the other side.

"He must be looking for a way in," Bunwinkle

said, "but there's only one way."

They both turned to look at the pet door.

Horace's jaw tightened. "This will not stand!"

"Yeah." Bunwinkle narrowed her eyes. "He's tangling with the wrong pets." She lifted a hoof. "Pet-tectives kick butt."

Her words were steady, but her hoof was not. It shook when Horace bumped it with his paw. He was going to have to talk to his sister pig when this was over.

Getting through the flap quietly proved challenging. Even when the Homestead was bustling, you could hear it slap closed. It didn't help matters that Bunwinkle caught her front hoof and crashed onto the floor, snout first.

"There's goes the element of surprise." Horace sighed.

"It's not like I did it on purpose."

A sound from the family room caught their attention.

Horace nodded his head in that direction. "This way."

They inched forward, slow but steady. Eyes scanning every surface and every shadow, sniffers detecting every scent. Onward they went, the intruder's detestable smell growing stronger as they neared their sleeping area.

Indignation flooded Horace's soul. "He'd better not be in our—"

Suddenly the creature sprang up from under Horace's bed, throwing covers everywhere. With a laugh he flipped over them like a gymnast and ran toward the pet door. "You'll never catch me," he called over his shoulder.

It happened so fast Horace didn't have time to react. He looked back at Bunwinkle. She shook her head like she was clearing an Etch A Sketch and said, "I don't know what that was, but it wasn't a raccoon. The head was too small, and the face mask thing is totally different."

"Whatever it is, we need to capture it."

Bunwinkle glanced up, then started shouting, "Hey, stop that!"

Horace's eyes snapped up to see the critter picking his nose and wiping it on the window.

"Good heavens!" he exclaimed. What a horrible creature. Shoo was an oddball, but he seemed good-hearted. This beast, on the other hand, was

rotten to the core.

When he looked again, the critter had turned and started shaking his hind end at them.

"Wait, is that a diaper?" Bunwinkle squinted at the window.

The villain did appear to be wearing a diaper. How odd.

"Hey, didn't we find a diaper like that in the trash?" Bunwinkle said "Does that mean he's tried to break in before?"

Indignation filled Horace's body. "It's time to put a stop to this!" he shouted. Then he leaned close to Bunwinkle and whispered, "You stay here and distract him while I sneak out and apprehend him."

"I stay here where it's safe?" Bunwinkle whispered back.

He nodded.

"Okay."

Horace quickly and quietly edged away from her. As soon as he rounded the corner of the couch, Bunwinkle began yelling.

"Hey, fur face, you're toast!"

The dancing stopped.

This was it. Time to move. Horace sprinted out of the family room and through the kitchen. He could hear Bunwinkle blowing raspberries in the other room. He took the doggie door slow so it wouldn't give him away.

Once he was through, he edged to the corner of the house and peeked around. The critter had turned and was rummaging in his diaper.

Disgusting!

But it did give Horace the opportunity to sneak up on him.

Unfortunately, the moment he sprang toward the culprit, the porch light flared, then popped, leaving Horace momentarily blinded. He heard him scamper away, but his sniffer said the creature hadn't gone far.

Horace was inspecting the area when Bunwinkle raced up.

"The roof," she panted. "He . . . went up . . . to the roof."

"Blast!"

"We can still track him." She lifted her snout up and inhaled.

Out of nowhere, the animal control van

appeared, and a floodlight came on and Samson's voice filled the air. "Where are you, little guy? I'm waiting for you."

They heard scrambling up on the roof and then a rustling in the trees.

"That's right. Come to level three—soon to be level two—Animal Control Agent Samson."

Samson swung the light in their direction, and they ducked down.

"What is he doing here?" Bunwinkle whispered angrily. "He's letting the trespasser get away."

"Right now I'm more worried about him finding Shoo. We'll have to let our home invader go," Horace said.

She nodded, then ran her nose back and forth on the wall. "Does your nose itch? Mine is tingly all over."

"My sniffer is fine. But it won't be if that dreadful Samson gets any closer."

The longer they waited, the more worried Horace became. What if the animal control man decided to search the property? What if they couldn't get to Shoo before something happened? Thankfully,

Samson moved on, and they were able to go to Shoo. He was exactly where they'd left him. When he saw them, he smiled and waved.

"My evil twin is crafty, huh?"

Bunwinkle snorted. "He's a big butt—"

Horace coughed to cover up the rest of her comment. He heartily agreed with the opinion, just not her colorful phrasing.

"Yes, we'll deal with him, but in the meantime, we have a more pressing issue. We need to move Shoo to the barn. It's the most secure location on the Homestead."

"We have to hurry, before Samson comes back," Bunwinkle said, rushing around to the other side of the trash cans. "I'm gonna push from behind, and you're gonna catch him. Okay?"

It wasn't easy dislodging Shoo. He was injured all over his body. The scrape down his back made it particularly difficult. As much as the raccoon irritated Bunwinkle, she was clearly trying to be gentle with him.

"It's okay, lil pig, push as hard as you can. I can take it."

Shoo squeezed his eyes shut and groaned as

Bunwinkle moved him, but he didn't complain once. At the last shove, Shoo fell forward onto Horace's back.

"Oof."

He was lighter than a piglet but still too heavy for Horace to carry by himself.

"Help!" Horace's legs shook with the effort of staying on his paws.

Bunwinkle appeared a moment later. "I got ya. Shoo, leave one arm over Horace's neck and put your other arm over mine."

"Sure thing."

The half-carry-half-drag method was slow going, but it worked. The plan was working perfectly. Until the other animals saw Shoo.

Blast! If Eleanor hadn't left the light on, they might have been able to sneak him in without anyone noticing.

"Ach, are ye bringing me a hat?" Mal asked as they passed his pen.

"No," Horace answered through gritted teeth, "it's a wounded animal."

"I dinna recall fighting a hat."

"It's not a hat," Bunwinkle grunted loudly. Her

voice carried, drawing the attention of the others.

The nanny goats took one look at the three of them and started screaming.

"Muuurder!"

It was a wave of chaos after that. The alpacas said something in Spanish that sounded like "peligroso." He'd look it up later, but he was certain

it wasn't good. But the biggest reaction came from the horses.

Jones neighed loud enough to be heard in the next county over. "No! No buccaneers in this barn. I will not allow it!"

Even Smith was distressed. "What have you done?"

They couldn't stop to answer. They had to get Shoo to his hiding spot—a stall at the far end of the barn—before Ellie got home.

"Guys, I can't stay here." Shoo squirmed until his arms slid off Horace and Bunwinkle and he flopped on the ground of the stall. "I've got a hay allergy. My nose will get all messed up."

Horace was about out of patience. And his own nose was having issues at the moment. "A mucus buildup is the least of your worries. The humans think you have rabies—if they find you they could put you down. You have to make do with this until we can find a better place for you or until your injuries heal."

The ruckus from the barn was getting louder. Bunwinkle shook her head. "I'll go calm them down."

That was a terrible idea. She was far more likely to make matters worse.

"Wait! Let me make Shoo a little more comfortable and then I'll go with you." Horace nudged Shoo onto his side and got a sneeze in the ear for his troubles. "Really?"

"Sowwy, I can't hewp it. Hay makes me . . . makes me . . . *achoo!*" Shoo sneezed again.

At least he didn't sneeze on anyone this time.

"No pirates, Horace!" Jones's voice echoed through the barn. As did the chants of "Muuurder!"

"I'm gonna take care of this noise," Bunwinkle called over her shoulder as she walked out of the stall.

Horace patted Shoo on the head "You won't be here long, I promise."

He didn't wait for a reply. The barn had gone silent, which worried Horace far more than the chaos had.

As he stepped into the barn, Bunwinkle's squeaky voice pierced the air. "Listen up, critters, there's something I gotta tell you."

Oh, no.

7

From the Horses' Mouths

The barn went quiet, and everyone stared at Winkie.

Good.

Awesome.

She had their attention. Now all she had to do was say something to keep them calm. Only she couldn't think of a single thing. Her mind was blank. And she was getting dizzy.

Maybe it had been a mistake to climb on top of the hay bales. Dang it! Why did this keep happening to her? She stomped her foot and shook her head real hard. She just needed to feel like herself again.

Horace's voice cut into her thoughts. "We're

here to investigate some suspicious activity in the area."

Everyone turned to look at him. Everyone except Smith, the black-spotted horse, who stared at her with a frown on his muzzle.

"It appears someone has been breaking into garbage cans around the neighborhood," Horace continued. "And even a few houses."

"You brought your suspect in here?" Jones cut in. "Putting the rest of us in danger?"

"No," she snapped at him. "We wouldn't do that."

"The raccoon you saw was not a suspect, but rather a witness. He's here under our protection." Horace climbed up next to her.

Winkie took it from there. "Right. We gotta keep him safe. And we gotta find the critter who did all these terrible things and—"

"Bring him to justice!" Horace had a fierce look in his eyes. "We can't allow a wild animal to invade our sleeping quarters and shake his back-side at us."

"Oh, good point, Horace."

"Did this critter have a long, striped tail?"

91

Jones asked. "Looks like he's wearing a mask?"

"Yeah." Winkie didn't want to get too excited. This was Jones, after all—he had a wilder imagination than the people who wrote the show *Meerkats in Space*, and they were super creative.

"Looks like a raccoon, but with a smaller head? Smith asked. "Wears a diaper?"

Horace glanced at Winkie. Maybe the horses had seen something.

"That's correct." Horace hopped down from the hay bales and went to stand in front of the horses.

Getting down wasn't so easy for Winkie. She fell a couple times, which gave her a headache. By the time she reached Horace, she was feeling kinda grumpy.

". . . out of the field behind the barn. Comes and goes easy as you please," Jones said, his ears twitching with excitement. "I told Smith, I said, 'Smith, that buccaneer is up to no good. He's here to kidnap us and force us into a life at sea. And I was right."

Winkie stared at the old gray horse.

Horace's forehead wrinkled and he tilted his head. "But why would pirates want horses?"

Thankfully Smith was there to clear things up.

"Weren't no buccaneer, you old crowbait." Smith shook his head. "It was . . . well, don't rightly know what it was, but I can tell you I ain't seen nothing like it before."

Jones's eyes got real big, and so did his nose-holes. "Call me crowbait, will ya?" He turned his head and continued, "Least I'm not a liar. Did you hear that, or have you gone deaf again?"

Smith looked like he wanted to bite his brother. Winkie knew the feeling. There were loads of times she'd had to stop herself from nipping at her brother dog.

"It'll only make it worse," she said to the black-spotted horse.

Smith looked at her, then back at Jones, then took a deep breath and calmly said, "There ain't no pirates or buccaneers on a farm. It was just a critter up to no good."

"Pirate," Jones muttered under his breath.

"Uh, thank you, gentlemen, for keeping our witness safe." Horace nudged Winkie's side. "We'll head out now and let you two continue your conversation."

On alert for the animal control guy, Winkie and Horace crept back to the house and had barely made it inside when they heard Ellie's voice. She was walking up the gravel drive talking with someone. Winkie and Horace rushed over to their beds but skidded to a stop at the same time.

"The door!" they said in unison.

They rushed back through the kitchen to the pet door.

Ellie's voice was a lot closer now. It sounded like she was at the bottom of the porch stairs.

"Thanks again for your help, Betty."

"Gosh sakes, I'm having a ball. I've been dying to make a line of Butters's Butter since I

was a kid. And the farmers' market is finally my chance." The older woman's voice was quieter, like she was farther away.

"Butters's Butter? That's a cute name," Ellie said.

Betty laughed. "Yes, it is. And first thing tomorrow I'll go visit the people who couldn't make it tonight and tell them about the farmers' market. Well, kiddo, I'm going to head home. Have a good night."

Her footsteps were loud on the gravel as she walked away.

"Quickly! Let's get the door down while we have something to mask the sound."

Winkie reared back, but then Ellie's phone rang.

"Wait." Horace put up a paw and stopped her.

"Oh, hey, Jennie." There was a creak of wood. Ellie must have sat down on the porch. "The meeting went well. A lot of people were interested. . . . Uh-huh. . . . I hope you're right. If this farmers' market doesn't work, I don't know how I'll be able to afford to keep all my animals."

Winkie gasped and Horace's peaches—the

part where his whiskers stuck out—lost all their pinkness.

"This is worse than we thought," Winkie whispered.

"Dean offered to buy the field, but I can't sell it. My uncle's will was very specific. I can't sell just one part of the property. If I sell the field, I have to sell the Homestead too, and I don't want to do that. I love it here."

"What are we gonna do, Horace?" Winkie's voice shook a little.

Horace stood up tall and looked her in the eyes. "We're going to make sure that the farmers' market is a success. And we're going to catch the villain who invaded our home. But first we're going to take care of this door so we don't get in trouble."

Lowering the cover on the pet door turned out to be a lot harder than raising it. Winkie wound up having to do hooves of steel three times before the stupid thing closed. It got super noisy, and Ellie was there in a flash.

"You poor things, you're probably dying to get out there and take care of business." She swung the door open and waved them outside. Into the phone she said, "I'll call you back later, Jennie."

"That was a close one," Winkie whispered to Horace.

He wasn't paying attention to her, though. He had his nose high, sniffing the air. "Do you smell that?"

Before she could answer, Clark Samson, the animal control guy, crawled out of the grass in front of them. He had some kind of goggles over his eyes.

"I got you now!" He grabbed hold of Winkie's leg.

She squealed and pulled back, but that only made him tighten his grip.

"Oh no. You're not going anywhere."

"Hey!" Ellie charged over. "What do you think you're doing?"

Samson released Winkie's leg and whipped off his goggles. "You're not a raccoon!"

This guy couldn't track his own head, and it was attached to his body.

Horace got between them and barked. It quickly turned into wheezing, though.

Ellie scooped him up. "You're going to need another allergy pill at this rate." To Samson she said, "Get off my property. Now."

When Winkie finally dropped into her bed, her nose started itching right away.

Great. Now her allergies were acting up.

She rubbed her snout against her hoof. What a day. Trapped under the house. Chasing the home intruder away. Rescuing Shoo. And to top it all off, Ellie wanted to sell the animals on the Homestead. It was too much for Winkie's brain. She needed sleep.

Horace was having some problems, though. "I don't know how I'm going to sleep, knowing that dreadful raccoon was in my bed."

"Just lie down and close your eyes. Besides, I got a good look at the trespasser and I don't think it was a raccoon. It was more like a really big weasel or something."

"He was definitely something," Horace muttered, and continued pawing at his blankets, shifting them around and around and bumping her bed.

"Stop already. I'm getting motion sick."

"It's disgusting," Horace grumbled. "I can still smell that horrible creature."

"I don't know how you can smell anything after being around the animal control guy." Winkie yawned.

He kept digging around. "I have an extraordinary sniffer, that's why."

Winkie was never going to get to sleep. Seriously, her whole body was itchy, but you didn't hear her complaining. Mostly because she was too tired to do anything but pass out.

"Do you want to switch beds for tonight?" she offered.

"That . . . won't . . . be . . ." He huffed and shifted and huffed and shifted. "Well, perhaps it would be best."

Winkie was too exhausted to stand up, so she rolled into Horace's bed.

Horace moved to her bed and immediately started pawing at the blankets. He turned one, two, three times, then settled down. Winkie breathed a heavy sigh. Finally, sleep time.

"Ah-hem." Horace cleared his throat. "Are you

feeling all right?"

Noooooo! Why wouldn't he let her sleep? Maybe if she lay real still he'd leave her alone. Which was easier said than done, what with the itchies starting up again.

"It's just that you've been acting a bit . . . odd lately." His voice got quieter as he continued. "I'm worried about you."

"Well, don't worry about me," she grumbled, and turned her back on Horace. "Worry about Ellie and the Homestead and let me sleep."

He sighed, then was quiet for a long time. Long enough for her irritation to fade and her body to relax. She was just drifting off when Horace stood up and said, "Ugh, I can't do it. I need my bed back."

* * *

It was a bad night. Winkie barely slept, and when she did, she dreamed of being locked in a cage. She woke up with sore eyes and the itchies worse than the night before. Horace lifted his head, smacked his lips a few times, then rolled over and went back to sleep.

For once she agreed with him. Winkie nestled back into her blankets, though she couldn't get deep asleep, thanks to Ellie banging around in the kitchen. How was it possible for a human to make more noise than a herd of elephants?

After about a million years Ellie went out to milk the goats. Winkie had never been so grateful to hear the screen door slam. Ellie would be busy outside for a while. Who knew, maybe she would even decide to clean out the stalls in the barn.

Winkie's eyes snapped open. Stalls? Barn? Oh no, she would find Shoo!

She jumped to her hooves and shouted at Horace. She meant to say, "Hurry, we have to save Shoo!" But her brain was going too fast, and what came out of her mouth was, "Ugh, shoes!"

Horace hopped up and raced out of the room.

He stopped at the door and hit it with his paw. Half the door fell off in front of them. "It must have broken last night when you did hooves of steel."

"It's okay. There's enough room for us to squeeze out," Winkie said as she stuck her head through the door.

Thankfully, Ellie was still busy with the goats. Mostly because the nanny goats were jerks and kept knocking over the milk bucket.

As they passed the goat pens, Horace slowed down.

"Act casual," he whispered.

They moseyed across the courtyard without Ellie noticing a thing.

As soon as they were inside the barn, they started running again. Jones called out to them as they approached Shoo's stall.

"Got something to tell ya," the old gray said.

"Uh-huh." Winkie wasn't really paying attention to him. Horace had just opened the stall door and . . .

"He's gone," Jones told them.

8

Making New Friends

Horace groaned. After all their efforts to get him to a safe place, Shoo had simply walked out.

"What do you mean he's gone?" Bunwinkle asked, outraged. "His back was all messed up. How did he get out of here?"

Jones leaned down and whispered, "Crawled out on all fours. Kept saying 'Argh' as he went. That's no ordinary raccoon, I'm telling ya. That thing is a bona fide pirate."

"Why didn't you stop him?" Horace could feel a headache coming on.

"How were we supposed to do that?" Smith said. "We're stuck in these here stalls."

Bunwinkle nodded, then pressed her nose

against the stall door. "I got the worst case of the itchies. Ever."

A look of pure terror came across Jones's face, and he backed away. "Brother, those buccaneers poisoned the piglet."

"Not pois—" Horace stopped. A powerful sneeze was building. "That Samson fellow must be in the neighborhood again." He fought the tickling in his sniffer, but it didn't do any good. *"Aachoo!"*

"The pirates got the dog too." Jones's voice wobbled.

Smith snorted. "There are no pirates here! And even if there were, they wouldn't go around poisoning folks. They'd make 'em walk the plank so sharks would eat 'em."

"Sharks?" Jones's eyes grew round. "It's worse than I thought."

Horace took a deep breath to calm himself. He shouldn't get angry. It was always like this when they came to the barn. Still, it would be nice if just once they could have a normal conversation.

"You don't know which way the raccoon went, by any chance?" he asked. "We have to find him before the humans do."

"Of course. He's at the pond behind the barn," Smith told them.

Jones whinnied loudly. "Are you trying to get Horace and Winkie killed?"

"Oh, hush."

"I have to get out of here," Bunwinkle said. "Feels like my whole body has the itchies." She waved at the horses and rushed out.

Smith and Jones watched her go, then turned their attention back to Horace.

"Keep an eye on her, Horace. She's not acting like herself," Smith said.

Jones nodded. "I'm worried."

Horace's heart sank. Even the horses had noticed a difference in Bunwinkle's behavior.

"Don't worry," he told them. "I'll protect her."

Unfortunately, there was only so much he could protect her from, and disgruntled chicks were not on the list. Horace walked out of the barn to find Bunwinkle arguing with Gladys, the smallest chick in the coop.

"No butt," Gladys, said stomping her tiny foot.

"No butt!" the other chicks echoed.

She glared at them. "Look, fuzz buckets, I've got an itch on my behind that is driving me up a wall. If I want to use the coop door to scratch it, I'm going to use it!"

Horace smiled to himself. This was more like normal. Well, normal for the Homestead anyway.

"It's a waste of time to argue with them."

Six pairs of eyes snapped over to him.

Not good.

"We should go find Shoo." Horace nudged Bunwinkle with a paw.

She turned and rubbed her side against the door of the coop. "Agh, I can't stop scratching." She held up her leg. "And look. I've got these red splotches all over my body."

"Good heavens." He took a step back.

Bunwinkle groaned. "I think I'm 'lergic to that creep who broke into the house. Do you think he's somewhere nearby?"

Horace's answer was cut off by a chant coming from inside the coop. "Wolf. Wolf. Wolf."

They weren't loud. Yet.

"We have to go down to the pond before they draw Eleanor's attention to us."

"Which pond?" Bunwinkle asked, suddenly still.

He sighed. "The only one on the Homestead. The one by the field." Fear poured off her, but they didn't have a choice, not with the mad chicken chorus going, "Wolf! Wolf! Wolf!"

"You know, that's a good idea," she squeaked. "But I think we should probably look for clues about the home invader first. We don't want to lose his trail."

"That would still take us to the field. Smith and Jones told us that's the direction the villain comes from. Remember?"

"WOLF. WOLF. WOLF."

"I'm sorry about this." Horace hurried behind Bunwinkle, put his head down, and pushed on her posterior for all he was worth.

"Hey! Stop that!" she called out.

He pushed harder. She tried to hinder him by digging in her hooves, but he was bigger and stronger. He didn't stop until they were at the edge of the pond.

"Big jerk," Bunwinkle huffed. "You didn't have to drive me into the muddy water." Her expression changed. "Wait, I think the mud is helping with the hives."

"Now aren't you glad—"

Horace didn't get to finish his thought. Without warning, something darted out of a nearby shrub and grabbed hold of his ankle. He was a rational, respectable Boston Terrier, but the unexpected touch sent him leaping into the air.

"PIRATE!" he shouted.

"Aw, dude, I knew this place had bad juju."

"Shoo?" Horace's rear dropped to the ground. He shut his eyes and let out a shaky breath.

Bunwinkle doubled over in the mud, laughing and snorting.

Horace turned away before he said something rude. He caught sight of a white tail moving through the tall grass on the other side of the pond. He sniffed the air—Princess Sofaneesba. How delightful!

Princess Sofaneesba was a lovely and sophisticated cat from the neighborhood, and their good friend. She emerged from the grass, her fur as white as snow. When she saw them, a smile lit up her face.

"Dear friends." Her voice was high-pitched yet soft. "I'm so pleased you're here. I was on my way to find you."

"Hey, Princess!" Bunwinkle charged over the cat. "Look, my mustache is finally coming in."

Horace sighed. Here they went again. Bunwinkle was obsessed with Princess Sofaneesba's dark gray mustache. It was truly a thing of beauty, and Bunwinkle was desperate to grow one herself. Horace had tried to explain that it was unlikely to happen, but she refused to accept it.

"Oh yes," the princess said, backing up a step and accidentally stepping on Shoo's paw.

"Agh!"

"I'm so sorry." Princess Sofaneesba noticed the raccoon for the first time. A frown formed on her face. "Are you all right?"

Shoo glanced up, and his expression instantly changed.

Dreamy. There was no other way to describe

the way he was looking at the princess.

"An angel." His forehead wrinkled, then smoothed out again, like he'd figured something out. "An angel with a wicked mustache."

Princess Sofaneesba's smile grew. "You think I'm an angel?"

Shoo nodded and dragged himself out of the shrubbery.

"Oh no, you're injured."

"It's nothing." Shoo's voice had lost its spaced-out tone.

Horace glanced at Bunwinkle, who rolled her eyes.

"It's not nothing," Bunwinkle said. "His tail's a mess. His back's a mess. And animal control is after him."

An idea struck Horace. "Princess, would you be able to hide poor Shoo at your house? We can't find a suitable place at the Homestead."

"I don't want to be a problem or anything," Shoo said, his face beaming.

The princess was clearly conflicted. She opened her mouth several times but closed it again right away.

"We understand if you don't want to take him," Bunwinkle said. "He's kind of a pain in the butt."

"Not right, lil pig. I wouldn't say that about you."

"That's not it." Princess Sofaneesba sighed. "I would be happy to help . . ." She paused and looked at the raccoon sprawled at her feet. "I'm sorry, I don't think we've actually been introduced."

He held up a paw and grinned. "How rude of me, I'm Shoobert." He pronounced it *shoe-BEAR*. "It's French. Do you like it?"

The princess giggled and put a paw to her lips.

Bunwinkle made a gagging noise and Horace did his best not to laugh. But as the two stared at each other, his amusement faded.

"So you'll take Shoo?" he asked.

The white cat turned her attention back to Horace, looking sorry. "I will hide Shoobert on one condition."

Something told Horace he wasn't going to like the condition.

"You have to search for Smokey." Princess Sofaneesba didn't quite meet his eyes as she said this.

Smokey was a deeply unpleasant stray cat who rambled the neighborhood tormenting anyone she encountered. In the weeks since Horace had come to live at the Homestead, she had become his personal nemesis.

"No way," Bunwinkle said, shaking her head. She wasn't too fond of Smokey either.

It was probably nothing. And yet . . .

"She's missing again?" Horace asked.

"I'm afraid so," the princess sighed.

Bunwinkle snorted. "She's probably hiding until her fur grows back."

Like Horace's sister pig, Smokey had been pet-napped by the Hogland twins not too long before. They'd shaved her with an electric razor in an attempt to make her resemble a lion. The results had entertained Horace to no end.

"I don't think that's the case," Princess Sofaneesba said. "She wouldn't need to hide from me. I saw her with that unfortunate fur cut." Tears filled her eyes. "I'm very worried about her."

Still lying on his belly, Shoo reached out and patted her paw.

"I know she's not always the nicest cat, but

she's still my friend. And she was genuinely afraid when we were locked in that cage."

What could he say? Disliking someone wasn't a good reason to allow them to be in danger. But how was he going to convince Bunwinkle to help?

"We'll do it."

Horace's head snapped around to look at his sister. She turned her face away, but he could see the stress in her body.

"Thank you, dear Bunwinkle." Princess Sofaneesba bestowed a radiant smile on them.

"All right, we'll look into her whereabouts," Horace agreed. "When was the last time you saw her?"

"The day Taryn, my human, came to pick me up from the Hoglands'."

Bunwinkle's ears perked up. "That was a week ago."

"And you haven't seen her since?"

The princess shook her head.

Where on earth could she be?

"Look!" Bunwinkle bumped him with her shoulder.

Horace turned to see Dean standing in the

middle of Ellie's field. "What is he doing?"

"We've got another problem," Bunwinkle said, putting a hoof over her snout. "I think the animal control guy is back."

"Little varmint, I know you're out here."

9

Mixed Feelings

"Get down," Winkie whispered.

Everyone dropped to the ground except Shoo, who was already there. Dean walked back and forth through the field, stopping every so often to

write something in a notebook. He must not have noticed them.

The breeze brought a fresh wave of Clark Samson's horrible stench.

"Oh, my." Princess Sofaneesba's nose wrinkled. "Animal control is back."

"You know him?" Horace wheezed.

The princess nodded.

"Then you know why we have to move Shoo out of here."

Winkie stared at him. "How? We're stuck between them. Any way we go, one of them will be sure to notice us."

Dean moved in their direction at the same time the smell got worse.

"I'll distract the humans while you help the princess move our friend here." Horace wiped his eyes on the back of his paw.

"We're going to split up?" Her voice wobbled at the end.

He nodded. "It's the only way to save Shoo."

"Nah, don't worry about me. I'm good to go." The raccoon gave them a thumbs-up, then started dragging himself along.

"Oh my gosh, snails move faster than that."
Winkie rolled her eyes. "We'll get you out of here,
won't we, Princess?"

The white cat put Shoo's arm over her shoulder
and said, "I wouldn't dream of letting anything
happen to Shoobert."

Winkie moved to help, but Horace stopped her.
"Be careful."

She leaned forward and kissed his peaches.
"You too."

With that Horace raced forward into the tall
grass. As soon as he got a few feet in, he started
barking.

"Time to move," Winkie said, taking hold of
Shoo's other arm.

The trip to Princess Sofaneesba's house was a nightmare. Winkie was convinced animal control was going to find them any second. She tried to hurry, but Shoo groaned if they moved too fast. Worry about Horace made her stomach hurt. She could hear him barking and Dean calling his name, but that didn't stop her from being scared. It didn't help that the route to the princess's house took them through the field.

The longer they were there, the more freaked out Winkie got. She jumped at every sound, and it got harder and harder to breathe.

"Is this where you were petnapped?" Princess Sofaneesba's voice was soft and kind.

Winkie couldn't make herself speak, so she nodded.

Shoo raised his head. "You were petnapped, lil pig?"

She squeezed her lips together. She really didn't want to talk about it, especially when they were in the spot where it had happened.

"The princess was taken too," Winkie finally managed to say.

Shoo swung his head around to look at the

white cat. "You must have been real scared. Both of you."

The princess nodded. "I was terrified at first. All I could think about was going home to my humans." The cat sighed loudly. "Sometimes I have nightmares about being trapped in that cage again."

Winkie was so surprised she almost dropped Shoo. "I thought it was just me."

"Have you been afraid to leave your house?" Princess's face turned pink as she spoke.

"Yeah. But I have to on account of I don't have a litter box."

Princess Sofaneesba blushed more. "Yes, of course."

"Do you get mad real easy?" Winkie asked.

"I'm so embarrassed to admit this—I destroyed a slipper that belonged to my human, Declan. It was his favorite and I tore it to shreds. I hid it under the house where he wouldn't be able to find it. But I'm certain he knows it was me. I feel terrible."

Winkie remembered something Horace had said. "I bet he isn't mad. I bet he's just worried

121

about you."

"I'm proud of you two," Shoo said. "Talking is good for the soul. It heals wounds, aligns inner mojos."

Leave it to the raccoon to make it weird. But if she was being honest, Winkie did feel better. Her stomach didn't hurt as much, and it wasn't so hard to breathe anymore.

Shoo patted her on the side. "It's all good, lil pig. You're gonna be just fine. I mean, look at me. I can't feel my tail and my back is on fire, but my harmonies are centered and my brain is free of—" His head fell forward suddenly.

"And he's gone again," Winkie said.

Princess Sofaneesba looked down at the raccoon. "Poor Shoobert. We're almost there."

They were quiet for a few minutes as they drag-carried Shoo closer to the princess's place.

"There's a little shed where he can stay. My humans never go in there," she whispered. "It's tucked away in the trees at the edge of our property. Animal control will have a hard time finding it."

Thankfully the shed was close. The hinges

squeaked when they opened the door, and Winkie cringed. That was loud enough to bring the whole neighborhood over. She looked around to see if anyone was rushing to get them, but no one came.

"Oh, thank heavens," the princess said.

They dropped the raccoon onto an old lawn chair cushion.

Shoo looked around. "Hey, do you guys smell that? Smells like . . . hostility."

Winkie snorted. "I think you damaged your sniffer when you landed on your head." To the princess she said, "Can you look after him? I have to find Horace and get back to the Homestead before Ellie notices we're gone."

The white cat smiled and nodded. "I'll take care of Shoobert. And Bunwinkle . . . thank you for talking with me about all that unpleasantness. It makes me feel better to have someone who understands."

Winkie nodded, then turned and raced away. In the opposite direction from the field.

10

Decoy Dog and the Dingbats

Horace counted twenty steps into the field before he started barking. He had to draw Dean and the animal control man away from Bunwinkle and the others, to give them time to escape.

As much as he hated making a spectacle of himself, there was no other choice. If that infamous New England showman P. T. Barnum could play the fool to earn money, Horace could certainly do it to keep his friends safe. He took a deep breath to steady his nerves. Then he woofed—which came out deeper because of his allergies—and leaped in the air. Dean was just a few feet away, taking pictures of the field with his phone. He turned when he saw Horace. His face had a peculiar expression—it might have been surprise, or it might have been guilt.

"Hey, little guy," Dean called. "What are you doing out here?"

Horace ran over, playing the friendly dog. He panted and hopped around and rolled on his back for belly scratches. As soon as he was certain of Dean's attention, he jumped up and dashed away.

Dean ran after him. "Wait, you shouldn't be out."

Excellent, that was one human distracted. Now he just had to deal with the other. He had a plan for that too. Clark Samson's unique stink wafted in from the direction of the road. Horace headed that way, making as much noise as possible. Dean kept shouting after him.

Horace leaped in the air again and ran into a wall of orange. He'd found the animal control man, or possibly a neon sign.

"Look here, pooch, you gave away my position. I am covered in reflective tape specifically to prevent incidents such as this from occurring."

From the far side of the field, Horace heard Shoo groan. Samson tilted his head and closed his eyes.

"The beast is injured." He raised his hand, which held a small crossbow. "This is it. I have to make my move while he is weakened."

Without pausing to think of the consequences, Horace launched himself at the man again. Samson fell backward, landing hard on the ground.

"Are you trying to sabotage me, Boston Terrier?" He cracked his knuckles. "Did the raccoon get to you?"

Just then Dean caught up with them. "Horace! What would El say if she saw you acting like this?"

The words hit like a slap on the hind end. Horace stopped short.

What *would* Eleanor think if she saw him now? Would she be disappointed? An image of Shoo lying on the ground, scraped and bruised, came to Horace's mind, and his heart filled with determination. Eleanor always told him to look after the other animals, and that's what he was doing.

Horace turned and narrowed his eyes at the humans.

Come and get me, boys.

It was a grand chase. Samson wasn't as fast as Dean, but he was more determined. The animal control man almost caught Horace twice. Good thing Horace was so nimble. At one point he stumbled onto the road to Barton Orchards, where Betty Butters almost ran him over with the Butters dairy wagon.

Where was she going in such a hurry?

"Horace, we have to get you home!" Dean shouted.

No time to worry about the Butters woman. Dean was right, he *did* need to get back to Eleanor.

Horace barked loudly, then sprinted back into the grass.

A few minutes later he raced passed the chicken coop and into the courtyard of the Homestead, Dean and Samson close on his heels.

Eleanor stepped out of the goat pen as they arrived. Horace paused when he saw her, suddenly nervous. He knew he'd done the right thing, but there was no way for *her* to know that.

While he stood there Samson swooped in and locked Horace in a death grip from which there was no escape. "This'll teach you to mess with the authorities."

"What's going on?" Eleanor set down the buckets of goat milk and hurried over.

"Your canine left your property unattended, ma'am."

Dean put a hand on the man's shoulder. "You can let him go. He won't leave again. I'll make sure of it."

He'd make sure of it? Horace sniffed, then immediately regretted it. The stench of Samson's cologne was overpowering this close, making Horace sneeze repeatedly. Eleanor took him in her arms.

"No disrespect, ma'am, but you need to keep a closer eye on your pets," Samson scolded. "I don't have time to round them up right now, as I'm in pursuit of the trash bandit turned home invader. Catching him would ensure my promotion from level-three agent to level two, which, as you know, is a very big deal." He walked away in a huff.

Once he was gone, Eleanor turned to Dean. "What happened?" Her face paled and she glanced around frantically. "And where's Bunwinkle?"

11

The Real Culprit

Winkie was not lost. She knew exactly where she was going, even if she wasn't exactly sure how to get there. The easiest way home would have been through the field, but it was just too stressful.

Not that this route was much better. It took her past the Summerses' place and the chattiest cows in the whole world.

"Ooo, it's a pig, is it?" said a light brown cow to her neighbor, another brown cow. That one smiled and called, "Cooie, what a sweet little pig. Don't ya think, Deirdre?"

And so it went down the line. Each cow said she was a pig and the next agreed. And they got louder as they went. Someone was going to notice her soon.

"Yup. I'm a pig. Oink. Oink."

The cows giggled. "Oink, oink," two of them said back.

"Ah, look at you, speaking pig now." The one called Deirdre nudged her friend with her shoulder.

Winkie picked up speed. She had to get out of there before they asked for the full language course.

"See you later, ladies," she called over her shoulder.

She was almost to the road when voices on the other side of the rosebushes stopped her. It was Betty Butters and Mrs. Summers, the owner of the jersey cow dairy across the footpath from the Homestead.

"It's a generous offer for our dairy. Can I have a little time to think about it?"

Betty laughed. "Oh, for gosh sakes, I don't expect an answer now. You gotta talk about it with your family. But I'd appreciate it if you didn't mention it to anyone else for the moment. I'm trying to surprise my mom."

"Of course."

Winkie shook her head. Betty was buying her mom cows? What a weird gift. She hoped Horace never surprised *her* with a bunch of cows.

A gate creaked, and Winkie took that as a sign to get her tail out of there. She was just creeping onto the front porch when she heard Ellie say her name.

Great, she was in trouble again.

It was some time before Winkie and Horace could talk about the day. Ellie lectured them for about a million years and Dean joined in—it was like getting in trouble twice. At one point Dean even said he was surprised Winkie could be so brave. It only stopped when Horace sneezed in his face and Winkie got a splinter in her snout from rubbing it on the porch steps.

"We have to do something about these allergies of yours."

What Ellie did was give them allergy medication and wash their beds and blankets. That guy Dean stuck around and helped her with the laundry. And when that was done, he helped her pick up the family room. And the dining room table. And the kitchen.

Horace watched him the whole time.

"I don't trust this fellow. There's been nothing

but trouble since he started coming around."

Winkie didn't answer. She could barely keep her eyes open. She rested her head on her legs and got comfortable.

Bits of Eleanor and Dean's conversation drifted over.

". . . broke into . . . last night . . . and the Summerses' house . . ."

Dean had a deep, soothing voice, perfect for putting pets to sleep.

"The raccoon . . . caught . . ."

They were talking about Shoo, but Shoo couldn't have broken in anywhere last night. He was in their barn.

"Forgot to . . . where did you find Horace . . ." Ellie's voice was fading.

"On the road to the Bartons'."

Wait, that wasn't right, was it? Had Dean just lied to Ellie?

Winkie tried to focus on what they were saying now, but her brain couldn't do it. It wanted to sleep.

Mmm, sleep.

* * *

When Winkie managed to open her eyes again, the sun was shining in her face. She stretched and smacked her lips. That was the best sleep she'd had in forever. No bad dreams. No whistling dog nose.

What a great nap!

As she looked at the windows, Winkie's forehead wrinkled in confusion. Wait, that was east, which meant the sun was rising. And that meant they'd slept the whole night. They were never gonna catch any bad guys this way.

Horace was sprawled out beside her. His tongue stuck out of his mouth and his eyes were half open. Winkie hit his side.

"Horace, get up!"

He hopped to his feet and swayed. "Where's Eleanor? Did that dreadful man do something to her?"

"She's fine. She's in the kitchen talking to someone. But we need to get going. We need clues and stuff, and we're not gonna find them if we're sleeping all the time."

"Oh, these are lovely!" Ellie's voice cut off Winkie's tirade.

They peeked over the back of the couch. Winkie recognized Mrs. Sam and Mr. Trujillo from the neighborhood. They must be talking about the meeting tonight.

He tilted his head. "Ah, I see Mrs. Sam has brought over some of those pretty necklaces she makes. Perhaps I'll take a closer look."

"You don't want to look at jewelry, you want to see if Mr. Trujillo brought you any cheese," Winkie said. Her foot slipped and hit the remote, turning on the TV.

"Welcome to *Weird and Wonderful*. I'm Sheridan Simper, and this is little guy is *not* a hat. He's an angora rabbit, and today we're going to explore—"

Weird and Wonderful. A furry scarf with eyes. The answer hit her like a rock. "Horace, the bandit—it's a lemur!"

"Don't be ridiculous," he sniffed, still looking at the humans in the kitchen and smacking his lips.

"It's not ribbetlous. It's for real. I watched a show about Madagascar and they showed all these lemurs because that's where they come from."

"Yes, but while Madagascar may be a natural habitat for lemurs, the Homestead is not." Horace put a paw to his forehead, like he had a headache.

"I'll prove it's a lemur." Winkie dug around in the couch until she found the remote control. "AnimalTV will definitely have a video of one."

It took forever to do the search on account of not knowing how to spell "lemur." While she searched, Horace sneaked into the kitchen. He came back a minute later with a smile on his face and a spring in his step.

"Yes, indeed. Very pretty necklaces."

Winkie rolled her eyes. "Are you ready to watch now?"

He nodded and she started a video.

"Well, I suppose our home invader *is* a lemur," Horace said after watching a couple clips. "But what on earth is one doing in our neighborhood?"

Another thought tapped on Winkie's brain.

"Diaper!" She jumped up and shouted. "The home invader was wearing a diaper. And we found one in our trash too. That means the lemur was here before. That totally makes sense, because my nose got itchy after I was in the garbage and when we went to get Shoo out of the barn."

Horace tilted his head and scrunched up his face. That was his "pet-tectives investigate" look.

"Wild animals don't wear diapers." The words came out slow, as though he was working it out as he talked.

Winkie jumped up and down. "But pets do— and pets have owners."

"Which means he's working with a human." He stood up and started pacing. "Bunwinkle, do you realize how serious this is? Someone is targeting the neighborhood. And they've trained a wild animal to help them. It's nefarious!"

"Yeah, new ferret tights! Do you think it could be that animal control guy, Samson? He's pretty fishy," she said. "Following Shoo and watching him while the lemur rummaged through someone's house."

"Indeed. And he's the human most likely to have an exotic pet like a lemur."

Something was bugging her about Samson. "Why would he do it, though? Why break into people's houses and use their computers?"

Horace stopped pacing. "I need to think like Spot on *Andie's Adventures*." Then he sat down and started licking his legs. Winkie didn't want to watch, but it was hippotizing.

Horace looked up suddenly, his eyes wide open. "Level two."

"Huh?"

"Every time we met that man, he talked about getting promoted. What if Samson trained the lemur to create chaos in the neighborhood in order to frame Shoo? Then he could capture the 'culprit' and move up to level . . ." Horace's face fell. "I'm starting to sound like Jones, aren't I?"

Winkie shook her head even though he had totally sounded like the old gray horse. "Nah. But I don't think Samson's the one behind all this. There's really only one person it can be."

She and Horace locked eyes. "Dean," they said at the same time.

Horace stared at her and she stared at him.

"Did we just agree on something?" he asked.

"Yeah, weird." She scratched her head. "But it makes sense. That guy has a bad character. Calling you little all the time and me chicken. Where are his manners?"

"Very true," Horace said. "Plus, he trapped us under the house. He said it was an accident, but I don't believe it."

"Me either." Winkie nodded. "He was probably trying to get us out of the way so the lemur could break in."

"Oh, very good, Bunwinkle." He patted her on the side.

It was kinda throwing her off being on the

same page as her brother. Oh no, was she going to start talking about New England and licking her legs now?

"But why?" Horace went on. "What's his motive?"

She shrugged and winced. Her shoulders were sore from carrying Shoo through the field. Then Winkie's ears perked up. That was it!

"The field!" she and Horace said at the same time. Again.

His face went from excited to frowny. "This is getting disturbing."

"Yeah." She nodded. "But at least we know we're on the right track."

"That's right. Dean wants that field, and he's been sweet-talking Eleanor so she'll sell it to him. That's why he's here so often. And why he's so nice to her."

"Yeah!" Winkie nodded. "He's only pretending to be her friend so he can get it and do something awful like turn it into a landfill. Like that garbage guy did in *Andie's Adventures*."

"Terrible." Horace's lips scrunched up like when he saw a duck, and he went on. "Dean must be pretty sure of himself if he was out there taking pictures and writing in his notebook yesterday."

Winkie tapped her front hooves. She'd just remembered something. "He lied about being there too. He told Ellie he found you in the road."

"The villain!" he said. "He won't get away with this."

But there were still some things that didn't make sense to her. "You know what I don't understand, though? How did *he* get a lemur?"

Horace tilted his head and frowned. "And another thing . . . why break into every house in the neighborhood?"

"Wait, did *every* house get hit?"

"That is an excellent question. We need to figure that out. We also need to find the lemur. He's got to be staying on Dean's property somewhere."

An amazing idea popped into Winkie's brain. "Let's do some recroissant."

"Do you mean reconnaissance?" Horace asked with only a tiny bit of irritation in his voice.

"Yeah, that's what I said, renaissance," she said. "We're gonna track down that lemur and make him talk."

"You know who else we have to track down? Smokey."

Winkie's shoulders sagged. "We did promise Princess Sofaneesba."

"Then let us begin with that unpleasant task and get it over with." Horace shuddered.

"Let's go!" Winkie turned toward the door, but Horace stopped her.

"Are you sure you're up for it? You seem to be having some issues lately."

Winkie wanted to ram him with her head. Why did he always have to bring that up?

"I'm fine," she said.

There was a loud thud, like something hitting the side of the house, and the sound of the twins' laughter drifted in.

Laughter. The twins. A duffel bag. Can't see. Can't breathe.

A warm body pressed against hers, and Horace's calm voice said, "Close your eyes and take a deep breath."

Her body shook, but she did what he said.

"Hold it in there for a second, then let it out again," he instructed.

144

She did it.

"Again."

As Winkie took deep breaths, Horace repeated the same thing over and over. "You're strong. You can do anything."

After a while, she found herself saying it with him in her head. As she did, the shaking stopped and breathing got easier. When she opened her eyes, Horace smiled at her.

"Perhaps we should get some more rest before we go out."

She smiled back. Horace could be thoughtful too.

"Yeah, I could use a nap."

12

Attack in the Shack

Neither of them really napped, though. Horace licked his legs while Bunwinkle watched a TV show until the twins left again.

They decided to start the search for Smokey on the Homestead.

"It's unlikely that she'd be here, but let's make sure," Horace said.

They checked all over, but there were only faint traces of Smokey's scent.

"Do you think she could be hiding in the chicken coop?" Bunwinkle asked as they left the garage.

"I'm reasonably confident the chicks would have alerted us to her presence, but we can check."

They ran into the princess as they were sniffing around the coop.

"Oh, thank heavens. I was just coming to find you." Her beautiful gray mustache twitched up and down. "Something is wrong with Shoobert."

Horace started to run before he realized he didn't know exactly where he was running to.

"Past the duck pond and around the cow path," Bunwinkle called from behind him.

What could have happened now? Honestly, Shoo was a magnet for trouble.

The princess passed Horace and led the way. When they opened the door of the shed, Shoo was sprawled out on his stomach. The ugly scratch running down his back was covered in a heavy layer of white paste.

Princess Sofaneesba quickly explained, "Oh, don't worry. That's an antibacterial ointment. It's helping Shoobert heal."

"He looks like he's turning into a skunk," Bunwinkle said, moving closer to sniff.

"Bunwinkle! You got it all over yourself." Horace frowned and backed away.

"Makes my snout itch," Bunwinkle said,

rubbing her nose against the closest thing to her, which turned out to be Horace's cheek.

It tickled something terrible. "Stop that!"

She rolled her eyes but moved her snout off him.

Suddenly Shoo lifted his head. "Hey, look, it's Boris and Honeysuckle. What are you guys doing in Catalina?"

Horace and Bunwinkle turned to look at the white cat next to them. She kept her eyes on the raccoon. "Poor thing, he's all confused."

When he heard the princess's voice, Shoo spun around on his belly to face her. "There's my beautiful feline enchantress."

Bunwinkle snorted and immediately put a hoof over her mouth.

Shoo threw an arm around Horace's neck, pulled him close, and whispered, "I want to tell her she's the only creature in the world for me, but it would never work."

It took Horace a moment to think of a reply. "Sadly, that is true. Because you are a—"

"Rascal." Shoo reached a hand toward the cat's face, then pulled it back slowly. "I am a rascal, and she is a princess. There's no hope for us." Shoo's head fell forward and hit the ground.

Horace bit his tongue. How had this happened? Shoo and the princess had only met the day before. Bunwinkle didn't seem to share his concerns. She was bent over laughing.

For her part, Princess Sofaneesba was thrilled. She put a paw to her cheek with a smile. "Isn't he just the sweetest? I'm so glad the catnip hasn't had any negative effects."

Bunwinkle stopped giggling and glanced over at Horace. "Catnip?"

"What a bunch of idiots!" a voice called out from above.

The four of them looked up at the same time. The lemur sat on a high shelf, smirking. "Hey, friends." He waved at them.

"That's why my snout itched. You've been here the whole time!" Bunwinkle stormed.

"Yup. And you guys were too lovey-dovey to notice."

Horace growled. "Come down at once!"

The lemur gave a nasty laugh. "I have a better idea. Let's play. The game is called eat dung."

And with that the miserable creature ripped open a bag of fertilizer and started throwing it at them.

Horace jumped back to avoid the manure and landed on Shoo's hand. The raccoon yelped and snatched his hand back, elbowing Bunwinkle in the side. She gasped and wound up with a mouthful of fertilizer.

She spat it out and shouted, "That is it!" Then she charged the wall, hitting it with enough force to rattle the whole shed. The lemur lost his balance, fell off the shelf, and landed on the princess. Not one to back down, the white cat used her claws to defend herself.

Shoo used the opportunity to grab the hooligan's tail with his good hand. The lemur screeched and hissed so loud Horace had to cover his ears. It didn't appear to bother Bunwinkle—she launched herself at the lemur, who escaped Shoo's grasp at the same time. Two bodies came rushing toward Horace. He ducked and got a hoof to the throat for his efforts.

"Oh, Horace, I didn't mean to—"

The rotten lemur somersaulted over Shoo and out the door. "Later, losers."

It took some time for them to collect themselves
after the battle ended. They were all a mess. All
except Princess Sofaneesba. She was calm, and
her fur was fertilizer free.

"How does she do that?" Bunwinkle muttered
to Horace.

He shook his head. It was impossible and yet

there she sat, lovingly removing manure from Shoo.

Bunwinkle sighed. "Can we go? I've got the itchies again, and I'm so mad I could spit."

They had no choice but to stop at the pond. Fortunately, there were no ducks. Horace wasn't sure he could bear the humiliation of being seen in this dreadful condition. While Horace swam in the water, Bunwinkle rolled in the mud.

"Hey, look what I found."

Horace watched as she rooted in the mud at her feet. When she lifted her head, there was a small silver angel figurine in her mouth. She set it back on the ground where they could both see it.

"That looks like the pendant from one of Mrs. Sam's necklaces," Horace said, "but what is it doing here?"

As he asked the question, he caught a glint out of the corner of his eye. Something had fallen farther up the path leading to the princess's property. Horace pawed away the dirt and found himself looking at an earring in the shape of a B.

Bunwinkle walked over next to him. "Is that

what I think it is?"

"If you mean Betty Butters's earring," he said, "the answer is yes."

"We've gotta go back and search that shed, don't we?" His sister pig looked ready to cry.

He patted her on the back. "It won't take long. We'll get you some allergy medicine very soon, I promise."

"Oh, hey, can you scratch a little to the left?"

After a few good scritches, Horace led the way back to the shed and pulled the door open. "Princess, I hate to disturb you, but I . . ."

He stopped short. The scene before him drove words from his mind. Princess Sofaneesba ran a paw over Shoo's head and sang, "Hush, little Shoo, don't say a word, kitty's gonna kill you a mockingbird. And if that mockingbird isn't dead—"

Horace cleared his throat, and his feline friend lifted her head. She did not look happy to see him.

"Yes?" she asked.

"Terribly sorry to disturb you, but it appears we really do need to search the shed."

Just then Shoo opened his eyes with a yawn. He stretched his body and glanced around at them. "Whoa, how long was I out? It's still summer, right?"

"Oh, good, you're awake." Bunwinkle squeezed past Horace and started rummaging through the straw next to the raccoon.

He giggled. "That tickles."

Bunwinkle continued to root through the straw.

"Seriously, lil pig, you gotta stop. What are you looking for anyway?"

"Anything out of the ordinary." She paused her search to rub her side against the wall. "Anything that doesn't belong in a shed."

Shoo nodded, then reached under his chest and pulled out a small velvet bag. "You mean like this?"

"Have you been lying on that this whole time?" Princes Sofaneesba asked as Horace took the bag.

"Yeah," Shoo said. "It was way uncomfortable too."

It took a few minutes for them to uncinch the bag and pour out its contents. Horace wasn't surprised to sort through a pile of small silvery items like the ones they'd discovered outside.

"Hey, that's Ellie's sewing thumb thing." Bunwinkle pointed at a thimble with an owl engraved on it.

Horace snorted in disgust. "Do you know what these are?"

The others stared at him, confusion clear on all their faces.

"Trophies. Souvenirs from the lemur's nefarious activities. He's obviously using this shed as a hiding place.

"Oh, he's a claustrophobic," Shoo said with a nod.

"Kleptomaniac," Horace corrected.

Bunwinkle giggled. "Bless you."

"Thanks, lil pig."

Princess Sofaneesba leaned down. "I don't see anything that belongs to my humans."

Horace moved the items around in order to count them. There were eight, including the *B* earring. Between the three of them, they were able to figure out which trinket belonged to which neighbor.

"I can't believe he broke into eight houses," Bunwinkle said.

"Well, we're going to stop him." Horace turned to Shoo and asked, "Are you able to move around?"

"Let me check." Shoo stretched his back several times, then stood up and tried to balance on one foot. "Back's still a little sore, but it's not gnarly anymore. That's thanks to my lady over there."

The princess smiled and waved at him.

"So wrong," Bunwinkle muttered from the corner, where she was scratching her posterior against the shed wall.

Horace had to agree. He would have to give Shoo a good talking-to. *After* they caught the lemur. In the meantime, he needed the raccoon's help.

"How do you feel about joining our investigation?"

13

Staked Out

Winkie couldn't believe her ears. Shoo and the princess were going to do a stakeout too? What was Horace thinking? What was next—would they do pet-tectives investigate? Hooves of steel? She'd go live with the goats before she let anyone else do her signature move.

"We have two objectives," Horace said. "First, capture the lemur. Second, find proof that Dean is behind the break-ins."

Princess Sofaneesba frowned. "Dean Royal? The alpaca man? But he's so nice. My humans think very highly of him."

"I'm afraid they've been deceived. He's a villain through and through."

157

"He tricked everyone," Winkie added.

"Now, Bunwinkle and I will watch Dean's house." Horace drew a *D* in the dirt. "That has to be where the lemur is hiding out. Since he hasn't broken into your house yet, Princess, you two will stay here and guard this property in case he slips past us." Horace wrote the letters *PS* about a foot to the right of the *D*. "It's also possible he'll come back here to the shed for his stolen treasures, so you'll need to be on high alert."

"What do we do if we catch the lemur?" Shoo asked.

Bunwinkle looked around the shack until she found what she was looking for—duct tape. "Tie him up with this. Then come and get us."

"Sweet plan, dude." Shoo put up a paw. Horace stared at if for a moment, then bumped it with his own.

Princess Sofaneesba smiled. "This is definitely going to work."

Winkie sighed. This was definitely going to fail.

Ellie was busy calling people about a meeting later that night. She stopped long enough to give

Winkie allergy medicine, then she was right back on the phone. A plate of fresh chocolate chip cookies sat in front of her.

"That's the second meeting this week. Ellie must be really worried about money. And she's baking again," Winkie said. "She only does that when she's stressed out."

Horace shook his head. "She'll be able to relax once we capture the lemur and stop Dean."

Winkie lay on the couch, chewing on the corner of her blankie as a thought buzzed around in her head. It had something to do with itching.

"Are you having problems with allergies?" she asked Horace.

He sniffed the air. "No. They don't seem to bother me except when the animal control man is around. Why do you ask?"

"It's just that I only seem to itch when the lemur is around. Which means that you and I are allergic to different things. Your sniffer doesn't like Samson's stinky deer pee cologne, and mine doesn't like the lemur's dander."

"And what's your point?"

"Well, dander gets everywhere, like your fur."

Winkie's forehead wrinkled as she tried to work out exactly what she was thinking. "So whoever was working with the lemur would have it on their clothes, right?"

"That would make sense, yes."

"Well, that's the thing—Dean doesn't make me itch."

"That doesn't necessarily prove anything. Dean might wash his clothes a lot or keep the lemur locked up far away from him."

Winkie gave him a doubtful look.

"Listen," Horace said, "Dean is behind this. He wants the field and is sabotaging Eleanor to get it."

"But why?" Winkie asked.

"To build his alpaca empire. He's not content with selling a few of them here and there. He wants to take over the whole vicuña market."

"What's a vicuña? "

But Horace wasn't listening to her. He was busy looking up alpacas on AnimalTV.

About eight hundred videos later, Winkie fell asleep from total boredom. She woke up when Ellie's phone started ringing.

"Hey, Gloria, the meeting is in half an hour. Is there something you needed before then? . . . Oh, I'm sorry to hear that. . . . Well, if you change your mind . . . Okay, bye."

Dean showed up at the screen door as she hung up. "Hey, El."

She sat down at the dining room table. "You're not going to believe this: Two more people canceled today. I don't know what happened. Everyone was so excited about it a few days ago. I even asked Clary to host so we could fit a bigger group. Are we going to be able to make the farmers' market work now?" Her voice shook at the end.

"Don't panic. We'll figure something out."

Ellie put her head in her hands as though she was going to cry. Watching her made Winkie's stomach hurt. She got down from the couch and went to Ellie's side. Horace was right next to her.

"It's going to be okay." Dean pulled Ellie up and held on to her hands. "I promise. Now, let's go to this meeting at the Hoglands' place and see if we can find out what's going on."

"Okay." Ellie gave him a weak smile.

They gathered up some pens and binders and left.

Horace scowled after them. "I don't like this. Maybe we should follow them."

"And do what? We don't have any proof, but if we catch the lemur we can make the connection to Dean." Winkie hopped off the couch. "Are we going to be able to get out?"

"Of course." Horace led the way to the back door. "I took care of it while you slept."

Ellie had replaced the flap, but the button on the side had been jammed. Horace lifted the door with just his paw.

"Very nice."

The sun sank behind the mountains as they left the Homestead. Winkie stuck to Horace's side while they crossed the field behind the barn, her heart beating super fast the whole time. Was she ever going to stop being afraid of this area? She should have brought something to chew on.

When they got there, Dean's house was dark, but the porch light was on. They circled the house looking for the best place to hide. That turned out to be a little spot between the compost heap and the trash cans.

"Remember to be on your guard," Horace said as he settled in.

Winkie's stomach flip-flopped. Great, now she was even more nervous. Luckily, there were lots of things to chew on in the compost heap. Winkie rooted around for a treat.

She found an old corn cob right away. It didn't last long, and before she knew it she was searching for something else.

Horace's focus never moved from the house. He sat bolt upright, ears on high alert. "Did you hear something?" he whispered.

Shoot, he'd caught her. She dropped the banana she'd been munching on and kicked it away. "I don't hear anything."

He sniffed the air. "Hmm, very curious."

Winkie tried to think of something to distract him. "Hey, should we sniff around for Smokey?"

"I think we should concentrate on catching the lemur first. We can look for Smokey first thing tomorrow."

They sat quietly for a while. Who knew stake-outs could be so boring and so nerve-racking at the same time? She needed something else to chew. While Horace's head was turned, she leaned over and grabbed hold of the closest thing she could find. Which turned out to be a packet with a big cherry on the cover. It smelled good, so that probably meant it was safe to eat.

This wasn't regular compost. It must have fallen out of the trash or something. Mmm, yummy.

"Ah-hem." Horace cleared his throat. "Let's go

over the plan again. We're going to capture the lemur. Make her take us to her human partner."

"What if—" Winkie couldn't finish on account of the fact that she was choking. She must have inhaled some of that treat.

Horace patted her on the back while she coughed and sputtered. "Good heavens. Are you all right?"

She nodded, and a clump of the yummy sand fell off her snout. Horace's paw stopped moving, and Winkie could feel him staring at her.

"What was that?" he asked. His voice was super calm, which probably meant he was super mad.

The best way to handle this situation was to act calm too.

"That's just some sand that got stuck to my face. No big deal." Winkie turned her head away and wiped it on her leg.

Horace narrowed his eyes. "It's not sand." He raised a paw and brushed it across her snout. "It's sugar."

Why couldn't he just let it go?

"Ellie has never given me sugar, so I thought it

was some kind of sand."

"Really?" Horace pressed his lips together so tight it looked like they had disappeared. "We have to get you home right now!"

What? No!

"Geez, I'm sorry. I didn't know eating sugar was such a big deal." A thought hit her. "Or are you mad that I didn't share?" She didn't wait for him to answer. "I'm sorry, I didn't think you'd want any. But there's half a banana you could have. I kicked it over that way."

Horace made a disgusted noise. "First of all, I do not eat food that comes from the compost pile. And second, you can't eat that much sugar. It'll make you sick!"

"You worry too much." She brushed him off. "I'm totally fine."

Although . . . she *was* feeling kinda weird. Her body was getting hot and it felt supercharged, like electricity was running through her. Winkie jumped to her feet.

Time to move!

14

Captured!

Horace was doing his best to help Bunwinkle, but she made it so difficult. Getting into the garbage, refusing to talk about her problems, and now eating sugar. Honestly.

Suddenly she jumped up and squealed, "Hi-yah!" Then she took off running. Horace watched in stunned silence as she sprinted around Dean's yard, her hind end swinging to the right like it was trying to get ahead of her front end.

No use fighting it now—the stakeout was well and truly over. There was no way the lemur would risk coming out with a tiny piglet banshee squealing loud enough to wake the dead. Bunwinkle raced past him.

They would be lucky if someone didn't call the police.

"Bunwinkle!" he called as she zoomed past him.

"Can't stop!" she called back.

Three times she ran by him and then . . . nothing. No running. No noise. No Bunwinkle.

Where had she gone now?

Horace used his sniffer to find her. She sat on the bottom step of the front porch, nose raised, eyes closed. He approached carefully.

When he sat beside her, she opened her eyes and smiled. Then the step they were sitting on began to shake.

"Oh man, gotta run. Hi-yah!" Bunwinkle shouted.

With that she hopped up and disappeared again. He didn't follow right away—the temptation to leave her was overpowering.

She's your sister—your immature, ridiculous sister—and she needs you, he told himself.

It was quiet again. What was he going to find this time? The answer was Bunwinkle lying on the ground in a fit of giggles. Her legs flopped around and drool ran down her face.

Horace sat down next to her and reminded himself that a gentleman would never sit on someone while she got herself under control. Nor would he bite her. Hard. On the buttocks.

Eventually Bunwinkle stopped laughing. Mud and grass were stuck to her body, and her face still had a fine layer of red sugar covering it. With a wild gleam in her eye she announced, "We're gonna get that varmint."

"Yes, but not here and not now," Horace said with a sigh. "Now we are going to go home and come up with a new plan."

Bunwinkle stood up and smiled. "Don't worry, big guy, we're close to nabbing that lemur." She tilted her head. "That's a fun word, huh? Lemur. Leeeeeee-muuuuur." She started hopping around as she chanted, "Le-mur. Le-mur."

"You called?" a voice sneered from the shadows.

Horace meant to tell Bunwinkle to run. He meant to leap forward and protect her. But he was so surprised that what he did was grab Bunwinkle by the scruff of the neck and hurl her at the lemur. It happened so fast he didn't realize what he'd done until he heard her squeal as she flew through the air.

Good heavens!

"That's it!" The ring-tailed primate emerged from the darkness with an arm around Bunwinkle's neck. Before Horace could react, the lemur had grabbed hold of his ear. "You two are coming with me."

Horace had no choice but to follow. The ruffian was surprisingly strong for a creature his

size. Perhaps he lifted weights. Even if Horace could have escaped, he couldn't leave Bunwinkle. This was all his fault.

"This is all your fault," she whispered loudly.

"Shut up!" their captor snarled, tightening his grip on them. "I've had enough of your trouble-making."

That was rich, a home invader calling them troublemakers.

He dragged them down a dark, winding path away from Dean's house.

"Where are you taking us?" Horace asked.

The lemur squeezed his ear again. "None of your business."

"But you live here," Bunwinkle gasped.

"Ha! Is that so?"

Horace sniffed the air to get his surroundings, but the lemur's scent was so strong it confused his sniffer. They were in serious trouble now. No human could see them, and no one knew where they were. Horace had to try something. Politeness had always worked in the past.

"Uh, Mr. Lemur, if I could have a word with you."

The lemur squeezed Horace's ear so hard it was bound to leave a mark. Then he said, "Stop flapping your gums." He turned to Bunwinkle. "And you—stop wiggling!"

"I can't. I got all electrocuted by the cherry sugar, and your grossness makes me itch."

"Enough!" The lemur snapped. "I've handled my share of idiots in the past, but you two are the worst."

Again Horace felt his hackles rise. How dare this vile creature insult them? After breaking into their home and touching his bed? Who was petnapping whom? He huffed in indignation, but the lemur ignored him.

"Almost there," he said.

Their abductor dragged them through a hole in a fence. Horace could hear cows not far away. That meant they were on a dairy farm. But Dean didn't run a dairy. And that Samson fellow didn't either. Finally the lemur stopped at the door of an old corrugated iron hut.

"I'm not going in there!" Bunwinkle cried, and she began flailing her legs. "You can't make me go in there!"

But the lemur could and he did.

The metal shack was even smaller than it looked on the outside. There was just enough room for a folding table and chair, a kennel for their ring-tailed captor, and . . . Betty Butters?

She looked the same as usual—a pink T-shirt with the words UNBEARABLY CUTE written on the front and a grizzly bear cub leaning against a tree, plus a pair of jeans—but her expression was drastically different. This was not a woman to be trifled with.

"We got it wrong again?" Bunwinkle grumbled. "We're the worst pet-tectives ever."

Who could blame them for getting it wrong, though? Betty had been very clever. Befriending Eleanor, offering to help with the farmers' market . . .

Betty took a step toward them. "Buddy?"

When he heard his name, the lemur let go of Bunwinkle, who immediately began scratching her neck against a stool. For his part Buddy reached into his diaper and pulled out a black thumb drive. Betty plucked it from the lemur's paw and went back to the table.

"Good boy. I'll give you a treat when I get back from crushing the farmers' market once and for all," she said, slipping the stick thing into the side of a laptop. She watched the screen intensely, then a nasty grin spread across her face. "Yes! This is it. I've got her." She glanced over at Horace and Bunwinkle and said, "Your owner is up to her eyeballs in debt. But don't worry, I'm about to make a generous offer for that sad little thing she calls a farm."

Betty pulled the thumb drive out and tossed it on the desk. "It would have been better if I had come by this information earlier, but you and Eleanor always foiled my plans. I really thought the rabies ploy would work. No matter. I have the information I need now and there's no way for you to stop me."

She checked her appearance in a small mirror on the wall, then left, calling out, "Back soon, Buddy!"

As soon as she was gone, Buddy threw Horace and Bunwinkle into his kennel and shut the door.

"Hear that? Your human is going to lose. After

everything you did, she's going to lose, and my Betty will finally get that land."

"You're awfully bold for a creature wearing a diaper," Horace couldn't resist saying.

A loud thump on the wall cut off the lemur's reply.

"Who's there?" Buddy called out.

There was no answer. He glanced between the door and Horace a couple of times. "We'll finish this when I get back."

"H-H-Horace." Bunwinkle shook harder than ever and her breath came in gasps.

What a fool he was getting into a battle of wits with the lemur when his sister was in the middle of a panic attack. He pressed his side against hers, which wasn't difficult considering the size of the kennel.

"Let's work on our breathing." He inhaled and held it. It took a moment, but then Bunwinkle followed suit. He exhaled loudly, then repeated the process. When he trusted that she would do it on her own, he said, "Remember, you're strong. You can do anything."

"This really helps. Thanks."

Horace sighed. She wasn't going to like what he said next, but he had to bring it up even if they were trapped in a cage at the moment. Even if she got mad at him.

"Eventually you'll have to talk about what happened, Winkie. You'll never feel truly well again if you don't."

15

I Can't Believe It's Butters

Winkie closed her eyes and did her new breathing exercises. Maybe he was right. Maybe she did need to talk about it.

"I was so scared, Horace." Winkie hated how wobbly her voice sounded, but she kept going. "I tried not to cry when the twins had me in the bag. I tried to be brave, but I didn't know where I was or who had me."

It was quiet for a second. Horace was probably embarrassed. He probably didn't want to be pet-tectives with a baby like her anymore.

She peeked over at him.

"I was scared too," Horace said with a sigh.

Winkie took a deep breath. There was more,

but it was hard to say.

Horace nodded at her. "Go on."

"What if," she whispered, "what if you hadn't come for me?"

"You would have figured something out, because you're smart and you never give up." Horace put his paws on her hooves. "And I will *always* come for you. We're family."

How could two little words make her feel so much better? They *were* family, and nothing would change that.

"Oh, that's precious." Buddy the jerk-face lemur stood in the doorway, slow clapping. "Where's my handkerchief? I think I might cry."

Winkie shook her head. She'd been so caught up in sharing her feelings that she hadn't heard the lemur come back.

Horace snorted. "As if you would carry a handkerchief. Only a gentleman would do something like that, and you are no gentleman."

The smile dropped from the lemur's face. "You know, I'm really gonna enjoy beating you up."

But he never got the chance. As he stepped toward them, the door slammed open and a guy dressed all in black like a ninja crawled in.

"Gotcha!" The ninja raised its head and smiled.

"Animal control!" Horace and Winkie shouted together.

"You thought you could hide from me, but no one gets away from Clark Samson."

Buddy laughed and punched the man in the face. "Give me a break."

Samson shook it off. "Is that all you got?"

"You're going down, human." The lemur charged, screeching loudly.

"Chatter away, beast. Those are the last noises you'll make today." Samson pulled out the tiny crossbow and aimed.

Buddy leaped at the man's face before he could fire. His shot missed the lemur, bounced off the chair, and landed in front of the kennel.

"That's not an arrow," Winkie said.

Horace shook his head. "I think it's a tranquilizer dart."

Another one flew through the bars at the front of the kennel, barely missing Winkie.

The fight between human and animal waged on. Buddy hopped on Samson's shoulder, wrapped his tail around the man's neck, and pulled on his hair. Samson spun around, swatting at his tormentor. "You won't break me, varmint."

He stumbled around, knocking things off the table and running into the walls. The shack couldn't take much more of this. Just when Winkie thought the roof would fall on them, Samson pulled a dart out of a bag at his side. He moved to stab it into the lemur, who saw it coming and jumped off. So Samson wound up tranquilizing himself.

"Wait." He dropped to his knees as the sedative took effect. "You're not a raccoon."

With his last bit of strength, Samson raised the crossbow and shot another dart. It missed Buddy, hit the wall, ricocheted—and hit the lemur in the butt. A few seconds later he was passed out on the ground next to the animal control man.

"What just happened?" Horace asked.

Winkie shrugged. "I don't know." Then their situation hit her. "Oh, no. We're trapped again." She took a deep breath to calm herself.

"Yoo-hoo."

Princess Sofaneesba waved at them from the door. She leaned back and called, "You were right, Shoobert. They're here."

Shoo walked up beside her. His eyes got big as he looked around the shack. "Whoa. That is some serious aggro right there."

"How sad," the princess agreed.

Horace cleared his throat. "I don't suppose you'd be able to get us out of this cage?"

"Be right there, dude." Shoo tilted his head as if he was looking for a way around the passed-out human, then shrugged. "Sorry, man." He patted Samson's leg and started crawling over him.

The white cat followed him into the shack.

"How did you find us?" Winkie asked.

"Cows," Shoo said, fiddling with the lock on the kennel.

Well, that totally explained everything.

The princess filled in the details. "Deirdre the heifer told us. The cows have seen this creature coming and going. They heard you with her earlier."

Winkie shot out of the cage as soon as the door opened. She stopped to stretch. So much better. Horace didn't look too happy, though.

"What's wrong?"

"We have to hurry. Ellie's meeting is happening

right now, and we have to stop Betty from ruining the farmers' market and getting her hands on the Homestead." He turned to the princess. "Do you still have the bag of trinkets?"

"It's outside the door."

Horace nodded. "Excellent. We need to get the thumb drive from up there. It's evidence. Can you do that?"

"I'll do that right now," Princess Sofaneesba said hopping onto the desk. "Horace, there's quite a few of those stick things."

"Take them all if you can."

"What should I do?" Shoo asked.

"Do you still have the duct tape?" Horace asked. Shoo nodded.

"Then wrap it around the lemur's wrists and ankles. We're taking him with us as well."

Shoo winked and pointed a finger at Horace. "Karma's coming for the big guy. Very nice."

Winkie looked around. "He's too heavy to carry."

"What if we dragged him on that?" The princess pointed to an old red sled tucked behind the door.

A few minutes later they rolled Buddy onto the sled and Horace got them situated.

"Shoo, your paws are best suited for this task,

so you'll pull. Princess, you walk in front and look for trouble. Bunwinkle and I will push from behind. Now, let's go."

"Where are we going again?" Winkie asked after they got moving.

There was small pause and then Horace said, "The Hoglands' place."

Winkie's brain spun as she pushed the wagon. Even though she'd talked about her feelings with Horace, she still wasn't sure she wanted to be around the twins. Maybe she could stay outside and guard the lemur. That way she wouldn't have to go inside and face them. But that was kind of like hiding, wasn't it? And she didn't want to hide anymore. Being scared all the time took the fun out of everything.

Before she knew it, they were outside the Hoglands' house.

Shoo stopped pulling the sled and said, "You know what? I'm gonna hang out in the shrubs so no one sees me."

"Good thinking, Shoobert." Princess Sofaneesba smiled at him.

Pretty soon he was out of sight and it was time for Winkie to make a decision—stay outside and stay scared, or go inside and fight the fear. She took a deep breath, and Horace's words popped into her mind: "You're strong. You can do anything."

"I'm strong. I can do anything." She took another breath, then walked to the front of the wagon. "I'm strong. I can do anything." Deep breath.

"I'll take this to Ellie," Winkie said to her

brother, then picked up the bag with her teeth.

He moved beside her. "You can do this."

I'm strong. I can do anything.

"When we get inside," Horace whispered, "head straight for Eleanor. I'll make sure you have a clear path."

Winkie nodded.

Betty was standing in front of the group talking about community when Winkie walked in. What a fake!

They made eye contact and Betty's face turned purple. The older woman might not have known what Winkie was carrying, but she had to know it spelled trouble for her.

"Gosh sakes, I'm so nervous I think I need to use the little girls' room real quick. You all stay where you are. I'll be right back."

Betty took three steps before Horace blocked her. He barked and growled loudly, drawing everyone's attention. Winkie scooted around the edge of the room looking for Ellie. But the only people she got a good look at were Mrs. Summers and a very old woman, who had to be Betty's mom on account of them looking so much alike. Winkie started to panic a little and then Ellie stood up.

"Horace, what are you doing here?" she asked, trying to move through the group.

Betty laughed. "Don't worry, Eleanor, I got him." She grabbed at Horace, but he was too quick for her and she wound up grasping at air.

This was Winkie's chance. She wove her way through a maze of human legs, but it seemed like no matter how much she moved, Ellie kept getting farther away. That was when she heard the high-pitched giggle of Linn Hogland.

"Pigella!" The little girl picked her up and held her close.

Winkie's stomach flip-flopped and she started to shake. No! She couldn't stop now. She closed her eyes and took deep breaths.

I'm strong. I can do anything.

"Bunwinkle?" Ellie's voice was close.

Linn sighed but handed Winkie over. That was better.

"What do you have, little one?" Ellie asked.

"I'll take that!" Betty Butters said, snatching the bag out of Winkie's mouth.

Several people gasped and everyone stared at the older woman. They'd never seen the real Betty Butters before.

Mrs. Sam grabbed hold of the bag. "Betty, what has come over you?"

"Maybe we should take a look inside," Dean said.

It took two people to pull the bag out of Betty's hands. Mrs. Sam opened it and poured the contents on a coffee table. It was quiet for a moment, then Mrs. Summers lifted up a thumb drive.

"Why does this have my name on it?"

Betty's face turned white, but she didn't say anything.

Dean spread the items out. "There's one for the Sams and the Hoglands, just about everybody."

"I don't know anything about those!" Betty yelled.

Ellie looked at her silver thimble then turned to her former friend. "Then why did you steal the bag?"

"I didn't . . . I was just . . . those are nothing. I was just putting together some profiles for the farmers' market."

Lars Hogland picked up the thumb drive with Hogland written on it. "So if I plug this into a computer, I'll find my suggestions for our stall at the market?" He leaned back and called out, "Anders, would you bring your laptop in here?"

"NO!" Betty shouted.

Old Mrs. Butters stood up, and everyone went quiet. "What have you done?"

Betty's attitude instantly changed from angry neighbor to stubborn kid.

"I did what I had to do. I sent Buddy to get

financial information on"—she waved her hand around—"everyone."

That announcement super upset the other humans even though they didn't know exactly who Buddy was.

"Why, honey?"

"You can't build a dairy empire without spilling a little milk, Mom. And you can't build an empire with one dairy. I needed to buy them all. I wouldn't have had to do any of it if you'd let me be a part of the dairy." She stomped her foot like a little girl. "You never listened to any of my ideas. You never wanted to try new things."

The old woman shook her head. "You broke the law and spied on our neighbors so we could make cottage cheese?"

"Not just cottage cheese, but yogurt and sour cream too." Betty stood up tall and straightened her shirt. "Imagine a line of gourmet cheeses, all bearing the Butters name. We'll be dairy queens!"

"But you're lactose intolerant. Just the smell of milk makes you sick."

"You promised you wouldn't tell anyone!" Betty cried as she burst into tears.

Dean stepped between the Butterses and put a hand on the older woman's shoulder. "I'm sorry, Bertie, but we have to call the police."

Winkie scooted closer to Horace and whispered, "You were totally right about that 'building an empire' thing."

"Yes."

"Only cheese, not alpacas."

A smile popped up on Horace's face and he sighed. "A kingdom made of cheese."

His expression changed when his paw got stepped on.

"It's too crowded in here. Let's go outside," he said, walking over to the door and pushing it open.

Princess Sofaneesba sat by the wagon, a fluffy gray cat next to her. Winkie's mouth fell open.

The princess waved them closer. "Look who I found."

If Winkie hadn't been seeing it with her own eyes, she wouldn't have believed it. The new cat was none other than Smokey. And she looked terrific.

The twins rushed over and scooped up the

cat. "There you are, Fantasia! We've been looking for you everywhere." Nea rubbed noses with her.

Horace looked as stunned as Winkie felt. No way was this the same cat they used to fight.

"What's up, creeps?" a familiar gravelly voice asked.

Oh yeah, that was definitely Smokey.

Winkie leaned close to Horace and whispered, "At least we don't have to look for her."

Shortly after that Clary noticed the lemur passed out in the wagon, and there was a fresh wave of chaos before animal control was called. Clark Samson stumbled onto the Hoglands' driveway a few minutes later. He took one look at the situation and plopped down on a tree stump not far from where Winkie, Horace, and Princess Sofaneesba sat.

A few minutes later the area was lit up with flashing lights. Betty refused to go without seeing her pet first. An animal control van showed up as the police wrestled her into the back of their car.

As the van pulled to a stop, Samson wobbled to his feet. The door opened, and a short woman with a big attitude got out.

"Clark!" she shouted. "Do my eyes deceive me, or is that the varmint you've been tracking?" She pointed at Buddy, who was still passed out in the wagon.

He looked down at the lemur, then back at the woman, then back at the lemur again. "Uh, yes?"

"Excellent work! Let's get the beast in the van and head back to base."

"No!" Betty screamed from the police car. "Not my Buddy."

The animal control woman shook her head. "When will these people learn you can't keep wild animals as pets?" She slapped Samson on the back. "You know what this means, don't you?"

He shook his head, lost his balance, and wound

up leaning against the van.

"You finally made level two. No more fieldwork for you."

Samson grabbed her hand and shook it. "Thank you!" He smiled. "I promise you won't regret this decision."

Winkie waved as they drove away.

Horace sighed. "Thank goodness we won't have to deal with him anymore."

The princess smiled. "Well, I suppose I should find Shoobert and return home."

"Psst." Shoo's hand waved at them from the nearest bush. "Over here."

"Are you ready to leave?" Sofaneesba asked.

There was a lot of rustling and then Shoo stepped out. He had a leaf stuck to the top of his head and a super-sad look on his face. "I've been thinking about that, and I'm not sure we belong together. See, I'm a rambler. You're a stayer. I eat garbage. You don't even know where your trash cans are. It'll never work between us, Princess, so I'm gonna go. But I'll never forget you."

With that he turned and climbed back into the bush next to them.

Princess Sofaneesba put a paw to her chest. "Oh." It sounded like she was about to cry.

Suddenly Shoo popped out again. "Okay, you convinced me. I'll stay."

Even in the dark, Winkie could see the smile on her friend's face.

"Naughty Shoobert." The princess swatted the raccoon with her paw. "Don't ever do that again."

He took the paw and kissed it. "You got it. Now let's get out of here before the humans notice me."

Winkie watched them walk away. "You think they'll be okay?"

Horace tsked. "I'm trying not to think about them at all."

Winkie giggled and snuggled closer to her brother dog.

"What will happen to the farmers' market now?" Ellie asked Dean.

He shook his head. "I honestly don't know."

As they stood there, a song began to play.

Horace's ears perked up. "Do you hear that?

It's 'Your Love Put Me in Time-Out,' Five 4 One's biggest hit! Where's it coming fr—"

"Hold on, that's my ringtone." Dean pulled his phone out of his pocket and answered it, walking a few feet away.

Winkie giggled at Horace's expression. "Dean is a Five 4 One fan? It . . . it can't be."

A few minutes later, Dean came back, a huge smile on his face. "You don't have to worry about the farmers' market, El. I found another group that wants to pay you to lease the land. It's a Renaissance festival troupe. I didn't want to say anything until I knew for sure. I've been out in that field getting measurements and taking pictures. That's actually where I found Horace the other day."

"You really did that?"

Dean nodded.

Ellie grinned and threw her arms around him. "You're the best!"

"Well, that was totally uncalled for," Horace said with a disgusted hmph.

Winkie and Horace moved to the far side of

the driveway where no one would step on them. The cherry sugar had finally worn off, and Winkie could barely keep her eyes open. But it took about six bajillion years for Ellie to finish at the Hoglands'. Winkie must have fallen asleep, because the next thing she knew Ellie was putting her on the piggy bed in the family room.

"Mmm, comfy." Winkie yawned.

Horace pawed at his blankets, moving them from one side of the bed to the other. "I'm glad one of us is comfortable. I can still smell lemur."

"It's your imagination," she mumbled. "Ellie washed the beds."

"What can I say? My sniffer is stronger than yours," he said.

She sighed. "Just come sleep in my bed. It smells fine."

He wrestled with his bed for a minute, then huffed, "I suppose I have no choice." He moved next to Winkie and snuggled close. "Thank you."

She smiled as she closed her eyes again. Horace took care of her and she took care of him. That's what family does.

Ellie's voice filled the quiet house. "Why is there a spoon missing from my centerpiece?"

"Told you she'd notice," Horace whispered.

A Note from the Author

Thank you so much for reading *Horace & Bunwinkle: The Case of the Rascally Raccoon*. If you're like me, you've fallen in love with Boston Terriers and potbellied pigs. But before you go rushing off to buy one, there are some important things you should know.

First, there's no such thing as Teacup pigs or Pixie pigs or pigs that stay small. All pigs get big, like 100–200 pounds big. Yeah, that's small compared to farm hogs—they weigh about 900 pounds—but it's still big. If you want to adopt a super-awesome pig like Bunwinkle, remember to do research and ask the breeder lots of questions. Or even better, adopt from a piggy rescue.

Second, all dogs and pigs may not get along as well as Horace and Bunwinkle do. Dogs are hunters by nature and pigs get hunted, which means you may have problems if you put them together. Not all dogs are proper and polite Boston Terriers like Horace.

Third, every kind of pet has specific needs, like diet and exercise. Make sure you know what those are before you adopt one.

P.S. While Shoo is awesome, not all raccoons are as friendly as he is. In fact, they can be kind of nasty, so it's best to leave them alone.

—PJ

Acknowledgments

Books are like babies, it takes a village to make them thrive. And I'm fortunate to be surrounded by the best people.

Chief among them is my husband, Neil, who provides endless encouragement and some of the funniest bits in the book. Right there with him are my sons Jeffrey, Zach, and CJ. Thank you for always being there for me.

I'm also fortunate to be surrounded by a fantastic professional team. My agent, Kari Sutherland, who is my champion. My editor, Kristin Rens, who is a joy to work with. And the amazing illustrator, Dave Mottram, who brings my silly characters to life.

Great critique partners are another key to success. Thank you to Namina Forna, Nan

Swapp, Celesta Rimington, and Britney and Jess Gulbrandsen.

What village would be complete without pets? Seriously I couldn't write Horace or Bunwinkle without the inspiration from my sweet Rosie and Rocky. And thank you to my mother, Ruby Gardner, for introducing Boston Terriers into my life.

And lastly I want to express gratitude to heavenly parents who guide me in all my endeavors.